"Skye, I want you to give some thought to the idea of marrying me."

Whatever she had been expecting him to say, it certainly wasn't this!

"Why are you asking me to marry you?" She stared at him with compelling eyes.

He raised dark brows. "You don't think it's because you're a beautiful young woman—?"

"No, I don't," she cut in forcefully. "Nor do I think that it's because you've fallen madly in love with me. Something else is going on here, Falkner—and I think it's time you told me what it is!"

CAROLE MORTIMER is one of Harlequin's most popular and prolific authors. Since her first novel was published in 1979, this British writer has shown no signs of slowing her pace. In fact, she has now published more than 145 novels!

Her strong, traditional romances, with their distinct style, brilliantly developed characters and romantic plot twists, have earned her an enthusiastic audience worldwide.

Carole was born in a village in England that she claims was so small that "if you blinked as you drove through it you could miss seeing it completely!" She adds that her parents still live in the house where she first came into the world, and her two brothers live very close by.

Carole's early ambition to become a nurse came to an abrupt end after only one year of training due to a weakness in her back suffered in the aftermath of a fall. Instead she went on to work in the computer department of a well-known stationery company.

During her time there, Carole made her first attempt at writing a novel for Harlequin. "The manuscript was far too short and the plotline not up to standard, so I naturally received a rejection slip," she says. "Not taking rejection well, I went off in a sulk for two years before deciding to have another go." Her second manuscript was accepted, beginning a long and fruitful career. She says she has "enjoyed every moment of it!"

Carole lives "in a most beautiful part of Britain" with her husband and children.

"I really do enjoy my writing, and have every intention of continuing to do so for another twenty years!"

HIS BID FOR
A BRIDE
CAROLE MORTIMER

~ THE MARRIAGE BARGAIN ~

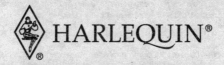

HARLEQUIN®

TORONTO • NEW YORK • LONDON
AMSTERDAM • PARIS • SYDNEY • HAMBURG
STOCKHOLM • ATHENS • TOKYO • MILAN • MADRID
PRAGUE • WARSAW • BUDAPEST • AUCKLAND

Recycling programs
for this product may
not exist in your area.

ISBN-13: 978-0-373-52722-9

HIS BID FOR A BRIDE

First North American Publication 2009.

Copyright © 2004 by Carole Mortimer.

This is a work of fiction. Names, characters, places and incidents are
either the product of the author's imagination or are used fictitiously,
and any resemblance to actual persons, living or dead, business
establishments, events or locales is entirely coincidental.

This edition published by arrangement with Harlequin Books S.A.

® and TM are trademarks of the publisher. Trademarks indicated with
® are registered in the United States Patent and Trademark Office, the
Canadian Trade Marks Office and in other countries.

www.eHarlequin.com

Printed in U.S.A.

HIS BID FOR
A BRIDE

PROLOGUE

IT WAS sexual attraction.

Pure and simple.

Except there was nothing pure or simple about the way Skye felt right now.

She was hot and feverish, knew her eyes must be overbright, her cheeks flushed, each breath she took painful with the effort it took to complete even such an instinctive function. Her breasts were pert, nipples hard with arousal beneath the fitted pink sweater she wore, and as for the heated desire between her thighs—!

She could feel all that—and yet she wasn't sure she even liked the man responsible for all these totally new, confusing feelings.

'Connor, I have no intention of selling Storm to you just so that he can break your beautiful daughter's neck for her the first time she tries to show off riding him in front of her friends,' Falkner Harrington now told Skye's father scathingly.

Falkner Harrington.

Arrogant. Condescending. Mocking. Handsome as the Vikings represented by that unusual first name!

Overlong blond hair, which should have looked ridiculous in this age of much shorter styles, merely added to this man's already overt masculinity, the sharpness of his features; straight brows over hard blue eyes, his nose an arrogant slash, sensual mouth twisted with derision now, his chin square and determined—all these things merely emphasized the man's untameable appearance.

Her more conservative father, in his business suit, shirt and tie, Skye acknowledged ruefully, looked more like a domesticated cat facing the fierceness of a jungle feline.

Her father shook his head smilingly. 'Skye could ride before she could walk,' he told the other man with dismissive affection. 'Falkner, I promised to buy Skye an Arabian as an eighteenth birthday present,' he added before the younger man could voice any more of the derision he made no effort to hide in that arrogantly handsome face. 'More to the point, Falkner,' her father added ruefully as he could obviously see the younger man's disinterest in such a promise, 'you and I both know that Storm's unpredictable temperament just isn't suited to the showjumping circuit.'

Falkner Harrington, at thirty-two years of age, was one of the top riders of the world showjumping circuit, and had been so for the last ten years.

But, as Skye also knew from numerous newspapers articles about the man, he was as much known for his prowess off the showjumping circuit as he was on it!

But, nevertheless, he had some nerve talking to her father in that condescending manner—because her father's whiskey company had been this man's sponsor for the last seven years.

She also didn't like the fact that Falkner Harrington seemed to see her as some little rich girl who didn't know one end of a horse from the other, merely wanted his precious Arabian as a fashion accessory to show off to her friends.

'Skye?' the younger man echoed mockingly, icy blue gaze flickering over her with scathing dismissal. 'With a surname like O'Hara, wouldn't Scarlett have been a more apt preface?' he added derisively.

The taunt, Skye was sure, had more to do with her almost waist-length copper-red hair, confined in a pony-tail at the moment, than it did with her surname!

Heated colour warmed her cheeks at this man's delib-erate rudeness; as if his own first name were so ordinary. Although, Skye had to admit, there was no denying how perfectly it suited his look of Viking fierceness…

'My eyes are a sky-blue.' She spoke for the first time, defensively, her voice husky, the slight Irish lilt making it more so.

Eyes of the same clear blue met her gaze with bold amusement. 'So they are,' Falkner Harrington acknowl-edged mockingly, that gaze raking over her with mer-ciless assessment now, taking in the rounded beauty of her youthful face, the pink sweater over pert breasts, denims fitting tightly over the long length of her legs. 'And you're almost eighteen,' he echoed sceptically, ob-viously finding that very hard to believe.

She was five feet six inches tall, not that short for a woman, her hair, when it wasn't confined, a mixture of blonde, cinnamon and copper, her skin, now that she had at last passed through puberty, pale and flawless, her figure perhaps a little on the slender side rather than vo-luptuous, but there was time for that.

There was certainly nothing about her, Skye decided indignantly, that warranted this man looking at her as if she were no more than a precocious child!

'Come on, Falkner,' her father cajoled. 'Just letting Skye take a look at the stallion isn't going to do any harm, surely?'

'No harm, no...' the younger man agreed slowly, still looking assessingly at Skye.

A look she deeply resented. If he would just once let her near the stallion then she would show him—

She drew in a deeply controlling breath, forcing herself to smile naturally—which wasn't easy when she considered this man had insulted both her father and herself in the last few minutes! 'I really would like to see Storm, Mr Harrington; my father has done nothing but sing his praises since he saw him last week,' she added encouragingly.

That deep blue gaze flickered briefly in the older man's direction. 'I wasn't aware you had been to see Storm, Connor,' he murmured softly—dangerously so.

Skye glanced at her father too, knowing by the slightly reproachful look he shot at her that she had just said something indiscreet.

'I happened to be in this area on business last week,' her father told the younger man with a dismissive shrug. 'You were away at a competition at the time, but your groom kindly let me take a look at the stallion you've told me so much about.'

'Really?' The younger man's relaxed demeanour hadn't changed by so much as a flicker of the eyelids, and yet his displeasure at this revelation was nonetheless tangible.

Skye didn't hold out much hope of the groom escaping verbally unscathed from this disclosure. 'Surely it's only reasonable for my father to want to take a look at something he intends offering to buy?' she dismissed lightly.

Falkner Harrington looked at her coldly. 'Reasonable, yes—if I had had any idea your father intended offering to buy one of my horses at all,' he rasped. 'Least of all Storm.'

'But why would you want to keep him if he's unsuitable for jumping?' Skye continued recklessly; goodness knew her father, as this man's sponsor, knew what it cost to stable, train, and compete horses who were suitable for the circuit, let alone ones that weren't in that class.

Falkner Harrington looked down his arrogant nose at her impertinence. 'Could it just be that perhaps it's because he's unsuitable for that purpose that I have my doubts about selling him to a young girl barely out of braces?' he rasped harshly.

The twin spots of angry colour in her cheeks clashed wildly with the redness of her hair; how could this man possibly know that until a few months ago she had worn braces on her teeth?

Skye could see from the corner of her eye as her father shifted in his chair at this visible display of her rising temper, but she was too indignantly furious now to heed that subtle warning.

'So you're unwilling to even let me see Storm?' she snapped between clenched teeth.

Falkner Harrington shrugged broad shoulders. 'I have no problem at all with your seeing him.'

'Then—'

'Merely with your ever owning him,' he concluded scathingly.

Skye opened her mouth, closing it again with a snap as her father sat forward slightly and lightly touched her arm. She glanced up at him, knowing her frustration must be evident from her expression.

He gave a barely perceptible shake of his head before turning back to the younger man. 'As you know, Falkner, I have a pretty impressive stable myself in Ireland. I taught Skye to ride there,' he added lightly. 'She really is a very capable horsewoman,' he assured the other man. 'Professional standard, in fact,' he added firmly.

That cold blue gaze flickered over her briefly before Falkner gave another shake of his head. 'We've already agreed Storm's temperament isn't suited to that way of life.'

'We'll settle for just seeing him,' Connor cajoled.

'If you insist!' Falkner Harrington accepted impatiently after a brief glance at his wrist-watch, obviously aware that he owed at least this much politeness to the man whose company was his professional sponsor. 'Storm should be back from his gallop by now.' He rose abruptly to his feet, at once revealing why he had looked down his arrogant nose at Skye's own height minutes ago; at least six feet four inches tall himself, he must tower over almost everyone he met!

Her father, a man Skye had looked up to and admired her whole life, looked positively short beside the younger man, even the breadth and power of the older man's shoulders doing nothing to allay that impression; Falkner Harrington had wide, powerful shoulders himself beneath the black jumper he wore, his waist and thighs muscular in cream riding trousers and boots.

The Falkner stable, as Skye had discovered for herself when she and her father had driven into the yard in their hire car a few minutes ago, was a large concern, and although the house itself was slightly run-down, both inside and out, the stables and training grounds were of the very highest standard.

Well, they would be, Skye thought disgruntledly; O'Hara Whiskey, her father's company, paid for most of that!

But as Skye accompanied the two men outside, for all the resentment she now felt towards Falkner Harrington, both on her own and her father's behalf, she realized that the sexual attraction she felt towards him was increasing to an almost overpowering degree.

The man was obviously lean and fit, his arrogant good looks beyond question, but it was the animal magnetism he exuded that made her tremble with longing, that made her aware of every aching inch of her own body in a way she never had been before.

But even those feelings faded to insignificance as they entered the cobbled stableyard and Skye fell in love for the first time in her life…

He was wonderful. Tall, dark, and so handsome he took her breath away, his face aristocratically beautiful as he looked down his long nose at her in arrogant query.

Storm.

Her father had told her the stallion was magnificent, pure black, with the fine delicacy Arabians were so known for, but he hadn't told her how absolutely breathtakingly beautiful Storm was.

'Thanks, Jim.' Falkner Harrington took the reins from the groom who had just returned from exercising the magnificent stallion, patting the horse's neck even as he spoke gently into one of the sensitively flicking ears.

'What did I tell you, Skye?' her father enthused happily beside her. 'Isn't he the most darlin'—?'

'Sorry to interrupt.' A softly spoken middle-aged woman crossed the yard towards them. 'There's a telephone call for you at the house, Mr O'Hara,' she informed him lightly.

'Ah.' He nodded knowingly. 'Can I leave Skye with you for a few minutes, Falkner? I really need to take this call.'

'Go ahead.' The younger man gave an abrupt inclination of his head. 'Skye will be perfectly safe with me,' he added tauntingly.

She gave him a sharp look before turning to give her father a reassuring smile, knowing he had been expecting this call from his older brother, Skye's uncle Seamus, in Ireland.

'You see what I mean.' Falkner Harrington barely waited long enough for her father to follow the other woman out of the yard before turning scathingly to Skye, Storm moving skittishly on the reins, the beautiful brown eyes glaring his displeasure at this change in his morning routine. 'Storm just isn't suitable for a lightweight amateur,' he added disgustedly.

'Lightweight—!'

Her father really wasn't exaggerating when he said she had been riding horses before she could walk. Her mother had died when Skye was less than a year old, and immediately after the funeral in England her father had sold up there and returned to his native Ireland to take over the running of the family business from his father, Old Seamus, taking baby Skye with him.

Instead of engaging a nanny to look after her, as most men would have done in the same circumstances, her father had simply taken her with him, either when working in his office, or in the stables that were really his first love.

Skye had been crawling under horses' legs, and put up on their backs before she could even stand on her own two legs, leading the huge animals about by their reins by the time she was two years old, riding out with the grooms on their daily exercise by the time she was eight.

How dared this man call her an amateur?

She could never afterwards have even begun to explain what prompted her into her next action, even to herself; she seemed to see her own actions as if in slow motion.

She grabbed the reins from Falkner Harrington's unsuspecting grasp, foot in the stirrup as she swung herself agilely up into the saddle, before galloping out of the stableyard up onto the downs she could see behind the house.

It was exhilarating, Storm responding to the lightest touch as he was allowed to do what he obviously loved best: running like the wind, his black mane flowing free, body stretched fully as hooves pounded easily across the grassy ground, almost seeming to fly as he jumped a hedge with effortless ease.

Riding Storm was the most thrilling experience of Skye's young life, and she knew herself completely lost in the sheer ecstasy of the moment.

So much so that she had no idea she was no longer alone until a hand reached out to tightly clasp the reins, pulling sharply back on them, Skye almost tumbling over Storm's head as he came to a shuddering, quivering stop.

'Are you insane?' Skye turned angrily on Falkner Harrington as he sat astride the showjumping horse Skye easily recognized as O'Hara's Lad. 'You could have knocked me off,' she accused indignantly.

He was breathing deeply between pinched nostrils, his face white with anger as he swung down out of his saddle, his fingers tightly gripping Skye's arm as he pulled her roughly from Storm's back.

'You little idiot!' He shook her roughly, glaring down at her furiously. 'You could have been killed!'

Skye smiled confidently. 'No, I—'

'Yes!' Falkner ground out harshly. 'Or Storm could!' he added furiously.

Which was probably more to the point as far as he was concerned!

But before Skye could make any further protest Falkner's mouth came roughly down on hers, the kiss he subjected her to owing nothing to gentleness and more to the anger that so obviously consumed him.

Nothing in Skye's previously youthful experiences with the couple of boys she had so far dated had prepared her for this thoroughly adult kiss, Falkner giving no quarter as his mouth ruthlessly savaged hers, his arms like steel bands as he moulded her body so close to his she could hardly breathe.

Just when Skye thought she couldn't stand it any more, that she was going to faint from sheer lack of breath in her lungs, Falkner thrust her roughly away from him, glaring down at her with eyes so pale a blue they were almost silver, breathing hard in his anger, every muscle and sinew of his body tensed with the fury that emanated from him.

'You're everything I thought you were earlier—and more!' he told her coldly. 'You're also completely irre- sponsible. Spoilt. Reckless. But most of all—stupid!' With one last disgusted look in her direction he swung himself up onto the stallion's back, grabbed O'Hara's Lad's reins, and rode off.

Leaving Skye high and dry, in the middle of the Berkshire Downs, with only her legs to carry her back to the stable.

Where she knew, not only would Falkner Harrington's anger be waiting there for her, but her father's as well...

But worse than any of that, she knew that Falkner would never let her father buy Storm for her now.

CHAPTER ONE

'JUST how much longer do you intend lying in this hospital bed feeling sorry for yourself?'

Skye stiffened at the first sound of that arrogant voice, quickly closing her eyes as if to shut out the man himself. It was over six years since she had last heard or seen Falkner Harrington, but she would nevertheless know that drawlingly confident voice anywhere!

'I said—'

'I heard what you said!' Skye turned on him glaringly, recoiling slightly as she realized he had moved from the doorway to stand beside her bed, having to arch her neck in order to be able to look up at him, so tall and confident in casual denims and a black tee shirt.

Sexual attraction.

In spite of everything she had gone through—was still going through—the frisson of awareness that coursed through her body just from looking at Falkner told her that nothing had changed as regards her total physical awareness of him.

Although the man himself had subtly changed, she noted distractedly. Gone was the long hair, flecks of grey visible in the much shorter style, his face still as aristocratically handsome, those blue eyes coldly assessing as his gaze raked over her own changed appearance. But there were lines now beside his eyes and sculptured mouth that hadn't been there six years ago, lines of pain as well as determination.

A week ago Skye would have known exactly what he would see as he looked at her, her hair cropped short now, the roundness of her face having thinned to leave hollow cheeks beneath blue eyes, her chin pointedly determined, and as for those voluptuous curves she had once coveted—if anything she was thinner now than she had been at eighteen, long hours of work having honed her body to perfect fitness.

Yes, a week ago she would have known exactly what Falkner would see as he looked at her, but she hadn't looked in a mirror for a week, hadn't brushed her hair or applied make-up during that time, either, even the gown she wore of the practical hospital variety.

'Well?' Falkner barked impatiently at her continued silence.

She gave a weary sigh, resenting him for making her exert herself enough even to answer him. Why couldn't he just leave her alone? Why couldn't everyone just leave her alone?

'What are you doing here?' she prompted heavily.

His mouth twisted derisively. 'Visiting you.' As if to prove the point he pulled back the chair beside her bed and eased himself down onto it, the stiffness of his right leg obvious as he did so.

Three years ago, Skye knew from reading the newspapers, this man had sustained dreadful injuries when his horse had gone down over one of the jumps, crushing Falkner beneath it, breaking both his legs, one of them so badly he had remained in hospital for almost six months. It was obvious from the pained way he still moved that the right leg, although healed, was no longer as straight as the other one.

Skye frowned her irritation at his familiarity. 'I don't remember asking you to sit down,' she snapped. 'In fact, I don't remember inviting you here at all,' she added rudely.

Falkner looked completely unperturbed by this rudeness, blond brows rising over mocking blue eyes. 'You have such a surfeit of visitors already, is that it?' he drawled mockingly.

She could feel the angry colour in her cheeks now. Damn him. How dared he come here and mock her?

'I'm sorry, Skye.' Falkner gave a self-disgusted sigh. 'That was unforgivable.' He grimaced.

She blinked back her sudden tears, angry with herself for showing even this much of an emotional weakness. 'A reporter, claiming to be my brother, got in here the day after—a few days ago,' she amended. 'He even got a photograph of me before they realized their mistake and managed to throw him out—'

'Skye, I know all about that. And the photograph appeared in the newspapers several days ago,' Falkner acknowledged heavily.

She shrugged dismissively. She hadn't seen the photograph herself, hadn't looked at a newspaper in days, but she knew it couldn't have been in the least flattering. She also knew she didn't care.

'Since then I've refused all visitors,' she told him woodenly. 'Which begs the question—' she suddenly realized sharply '—how did you manage to get in?' She frowned suspiciously.

Falkner grinned. 'By using my natural charm and diplomacy?'

Skye gave a disbelieving snort; she wasn't aware this man had any natural charm, let alone diplomacy.

'I asked you a question when I arrived, Skye,' Falkner reminded briskly. 'You're over the concussion, and your broken ribs are mending nicely, so isn't it time you checked out of here?'

She glared at him resentfully. 'I wasn't aware a medical degree was one of your many accomplishments!'

Skye was totally aware that since the accident that had excluded him from the showjumping circuit three years ago this man had turned his hand to playing the stock market, that everything he touched seemed to turn to gold. Maybe he should have been named Midas rather than the unusual Falkner!

'You might be surprised at some of my "accomplishments",' he bit back tersely, before instantly making a visible effort to relax. 'Although a medical degree isn't amongst them,' he conceded dryly. 'The truth is, I had a lengthy conversation with your doctor before I came in here—'

'You had no right—'

'I have every right, Skye,' Falkner harshly cut in on her indignation, sitting forward slightly on the chair. 'Skye, I realize that I'm probably the last person you expected to see today, that you wanted to see,' he accepted heavily. 'But the fact of the matter is—' He broke off, running an agitated hand through the blond thickness of his hair.

'The fact of the matter is…?' Skye prompted warily, suddenly extremely suspicious of Falkner's motive for being here.

She personally hadn't seen this man since that day over six years ago, but she knew that her father had continued to have a working relationship with the younger man until the time of the accident three years ago, that her father's liking and respect for Falkner had deepened as he'd first fought his way back from his horrendous injuries, to move on to make a success of himself in another field.

Her father...

Pain shot through her like a knife just at the thought of him, once again closing her eyes, although she couldn't manage to shut out the memories that had brought her to this point in time.

When had everything begun to go wrong for them? She had lain here this last week trying to make sense of it all.

There was no denying it had been a bad year for all the O'Hara family. Uncle Seamus's wife had walked out on him after five years of marriage. Uncle Seamus had always been a little too fond of the family product, and his drinking bouts had become more frequent, usually ending in blazing rows, if not actually fisticuffs, with his younger brother, Connor. But with Skye's help that situation had eventually calmed down, Uncle Seamus apologetic and shame-faced, the two men, to Skye's relief, once again friends.

Only for something even more disastrous to follow.

Six months ago O'Hara Whiskey had been in serious financial difficulty, rumours quickly following of her father's possible misconduct.

And then had come the worst blow of all. That fatal night a week ago...

It had been late at night as Skye and her father had driven back to their London hotel after yet another unsuccessful business meeting in the south of England, the rain beating blindingly against the windscreen, visibility almost nil. So much so that her father hadn't seen the truck coming the other way, hadn't realized it was driving on the wrong side of the road, either. Until it had been too late…

Her face was now as white as the pillow she lay back on, her eyes still haunted by those last terrible moments as she once again looked at Falkner. 'Would you please just go away and leave me alone?' she pleaded brokenly.

He reached out a hand to her, that hand dropping ineffectually onto the bed as she flinched away from him. 'Skye, I know how it feels to be in pain. Who should know better than me?' he rasped harshly. 'But I—hell, I wish there was an easy way to say this, but ultimately I know that there isn't.' He shook his head impatiently. 'You know they held the inquest three days ago?'

Skye nodded her head without turning. She had given her statement to the police several days ago—she couldn't remember how many days, they all seemed to have merged into one big, painful blur—knew that a verdict of 'accidental death' had been decided upon.

'Skye, your father's funeral is arranged for the end of this week,' Falkner told her gently.

No!

All the memories, those terrible final moments, fell in on top of her, her father's warning cry as he'd swerved to avoid the oncoming truck, the terrible sound as the two vehicles had collided, the eerie silence that had followed.

Skye had regained consciousness as someone, a stranger, had pulled her from the car, the pain in her head and side so extreme that she'd thought she might faint again. Except…

'My father,' she had cried as she'd sat up. 'You have to help my father.'

But even as she'd called out she had known it was already too late for her father, his side of the car completely crushed where he had swerved to avoid the collision, making it impossible to believe that anyone could have survived in such a tangled mess.

And no one had…

At the hospital there had been even more strangers to reassure her that her father's death would have been instantaneous. That he wouldn't have known anything about it. Finally, when it had become apparent that Skye's grief was inconsolable, that his injuries had been such that it was a blessing he hadn't survived.

A blessing.

How could it possibly be 'a blessing' that her father, the person she loved most in the whole world, had died so suddenly, so tragically?

And now Falkner Harrington, yet another stranger, had come to tell her that her father was to be buried in four days' time…

Skye didn't even glance at Falkner now. 'Go away,' she told him.

'I can't do that,' he told her regretfully. 'And one day you'll thank me for not doing so—'

'I doubt that very much,' she snapped.

'Skye, in four days' time, at his own request, your father is being laid to rest beside your mother, and I'm here to take you home—'

'I'm not going to any funeral, in four days, or any other time!' She turned on him fiercely, eyes blazing deeply blue as she attempted to sit up, the pain in her head and side instantly pulling her back down again.

'I'm not going, Falkner,' she repeated flatly as she turned away.

'Oh, yes, you are,' he told her firmly as he stood up to tower over her. 'You know, as well as I do, that it was always your father's wish to be buried beside your mother in Windsor. Skye,' he groaned as she looked even more stricken as he once again mentioned the childhood loss of her mother, 'I admit, I can't even begin to take in the enormity of how you feel at the moment—my own parents are, thankfully, still both very much alive and living in Florida. But I have lost a very dear friend, a friend that I'm going to miss very much,' he murmured huskily. 'I also know that dear friend would have wanted me to look after his daughter,' he added softly.

Skye's expression was scathing as she turned to him. 'If you're such a "friend", then where were you this last six months, when my father so obviously needed all the friends he had?'

Falkner straightened, his expression enigmatically unreadable. 'I was there, Skye—'

'I didn't see you,' she scorned.

'But I saw you,' he assured her quietly.

Her eyes widened incredulously. 'When? Where?'

He shook his head. 'It doesn't matter,' he dismissed. 'What matters right now is that I get you out of here with the minimum amount of fuss. There are still re- porters hanging around at the front of the hospital, so I suggest—'

'Falkner, I believe I've made my feelings more than clear on this subject, but just in case I haven't—'

'You have,' he assured her dryly. 'But that doesn't change the fact that you are well enough to be discharged—more than well enough, if the specialist is to be believed,' he added derisively. 'Skye, they need the bed—you don't,' he added impatiently as she would have argued with him once again. 'So let's get you dressed—'

'I don't have any clothes,' she cut in flatly. 'What I was wearing—' She swallowed hard. 'What I was wearing was in such a mess once they had cut if off me that I told them to incinerate it.'

'It doesn't matter; I have the things with me that you left at the hotel,' Falkner dismissed easily, turning to pick up the suitcase Skye hadn't noticed him place just inside the door when he'd come in, swinging it up awkwardly onto the bottom of the bed to open up the lid.

Skye gasped as she easily recognized her own clothes neatly folded inside. And just as easily guessed who must have taken them out of the drawers and wardrobe at the hotel before folding them so neatly and putting them inside the suitcase.

She shook her head dazedly. 'Falkner, don't you think you've taken rather a lot on yourself by getting involved in this way? I take it it was you who—who organized the funeral, too?' she accused.

His head snapped up challengingly. 'Who else was going to do it?' he rasped. 'You? Somehow I don't think so. Your uncle Seamus?'

He shook his head grimly. 'Skye, last weekend, after your uncle Seamus was informed of the accident, he went on the bender to end all benders. Your father's housekeeper found him at the bottom of the stairs the next morning, still blind drunk. Which was perhaps as well, because it turned out he had broken his leg when he fell down the stairs!' he concluded disgustedly.

Skye stared at him. She had been expecting her uncle

Seamus to arrive all week. Although part of her was relieved when he hadn't, knowing she would have found it hard to cope with his grief as well as her own. But listening to Falkner's explanation of exactly why her uncle hadn't come to England following the accident…

'I know.' Falkner sighed ruefully at her slightly dazed expression. 'If it wasn't so damned tragic, it would be laughable!'

He was right, it would. In fact, Skye was having trouble not laughing, hysterically, anyway.

Falkner shook his head before turning his attention back to the contents of her suitcase. 'They should be letting him out of hospital too by the end of the week,' he informed her distractedly.

But not time enough for him to attend her father's funeral in England, Skye realized…

'Here, let me do that.' She dismissed Falkner's attempts to choose something for her to wear from the contents of the suitcase; he might, through necessity, have packed these things for her at the hotel, but there was something not quite right about watching him handle her silky underwear. 'Perhaps if you would like to wait outside…?' she suggested huskily as she moved gingerly to sit up on the side of the bed, not quite able to look at Falkner as she was struck by a sudden—unaccustomed—shyness.

She was twenty-four years old, had spent all of her childhood and most of her adult life, too, surrounded by men; her father, her grandfather, Uncle Seamus, the grooms at the stable, the majority of workers at O'Hara Whiskey having been men too. But because she had accompanied her father since she was a very young child, she had always been treated by them all as 'one of the boys'; certainly none of them had ever made her completely aware of her own femininity. In the way that Falkner had six years ago. And, amazingly, still did…

Falkner gave the ghost of a smile. 'If you think you can manage…?'

No doubt it would take her some time; she knew she must look a mess, wanted to shower and wash her hair in the adjoining bathroom before putting on clean clothes. Which wouldn't be easy when her head still felt as if it didn't quite belong on her shoulders, her broken ribs making any movement painful. But slow was certainly preferable to having Falkner offer to help dress her.

Besides, despite what Falkner might have implied on his arrival, she hadn't spent all of the last week lying around in bed feeling sorry for herself, had been walking about the room, and into the adjoining bathroom, for several days now.

It was what awaited her outside this room that Skye was having trouble facing up to…

Somehow, cocooned inside the clinical atmosphere of the hospital, with no responsibilities except to take her medicine when instructed, and eat the food that was placed in front of her, she had made this her reality, what had happened the previous week becoming artificial, the previous six months before that dreamlike. But she knew only too well that once she stepped outside this room…!

'I can manage,' she assured Falkner abruptly. 'Thank you,' she added belatedly.

He nodded in brief acknowledgement of this slight softening on her part. 'Take your time. I'll go and get myself a coffee in the waiting-room down the hallway.' He turned away, the permanent damage to his right leg becoming more apparent as he moved awkwardly across the room.

He had moved so gracefully six years ago, Skye

recalled frowningly, each movement fluid and purpose-ful. She wondered if the leg still pained him. Although she knew just from their brief meeting six years ago that he wouldn't welcome her curiosity. Or her pity.

'Falkner,' she called after him, her voice quivering with uncertainty now.

He glanced back at her, his hand already on the door handle. 'Yes?' His own tone was almost wary.

Skye moistened dry lips before answering. 'You mentioned earlier that you were—you were taking me home,' she reminded him frowningly.

'I did.' He nodded abruptly. 'To my home, Skye. I'm taking you to my home,' he repeated firmly, his gaze challenging, as if he were already prepared for her to argue with him.

He was taking her to that run-down house of mellow stone, set in its acres of beautiful countryside, with its stables now empty of the most beautiful horses Skye had ever seen…

'Fine.' Skye nodded slowly. 'That's absolutely fine,' she repeated evenly.

Falkner looked at her for several long, searching seconds, before giving an abrupt nod of his head. 'I'll be waiting down the corridor when you're ready to leave,' he repeated softly. 'And don't worry about the re-porters outside; I've already arranged for us to leave by a staff entrance.'

'Thank you.' Her smile was tremulous, although she already accepted that Falkner seemed able to 'arrange' most things he set his mind to.

She could imagine nothing worse than a repeat of the incident when, by subterfuge, a reporter had managed to gain entrance to her room earlier in the week, the man's camera clicking in her face even as he fired questions at her. Questions that Skye still remembered with horror.

'You're more than welcome,' Falkner assured her quietly before closing the door softly behind him as he left the room.

Skye didn't move for several seconds, couldn't move, totally overwhelmed at this kindness from a man she hadn't believed, six years ago, was capable of the emotion.

A man she had been totally in love with for those six years.

CHAPTER TWO

'FALKNER, exactly why are you doing this?' Skye asked wearily.

She had taken one look in the mirror when she'd entered the bathroom earlier, and groaned with dismay at her appearance; it was worse than she had thought.

Her hair stuck up in greasy spikes, there was a huge bruise down the left side of her face where she had been thrown against the car door—also the reason for her concussion—her black eye had turned to all the colours of the rainbow but predominantly a sickly yellow, her face otherwise deathly pale. She had also lost weight, she discovered when she pulled on denims and a black tee shirt, the clothes much looser on her than they had been a week ago.

One thing she was sure of: Falkner wasn't being kind to her because he was overwhelmed by her beauty.

He glanced at her only briefly as she sat beside him in the green Range Rover, Skye having tactfully turned away minutes ago as he'd levered himself awkwardly behind the wheel. 'Would you have preferred it if I had left you to face those reporters on your own?' he rasped grimly.

Despite his precaution of taking her out of the hospital through a staff entrance, a couple of enterprising reporters had pre-empted them, Falkner's hand tightly gripping Skye's arm as he'd pushed his way forcefully by them to see her safely seated in his car before, his mouth a grimly set line, he'd moved round the vehicle to get in beside her, answering none of the questions fired at them.

'No,' she sighed, exhausted by the events of the morning, her ribs aching painfully from this unaccustomed activity. 'But—'

'I told you, Connor was my friend,' Falkner bit out abruptly. 'He would want me to take care of you.'

Before the suspicion and gossip of the last six months, her father had appeared to have many friends, but most of them had quietly faded away the last few months, almost as if they believed the rumour and speculation that now surrounded Connor's professional reputation might be catching.

Although Falkner didn't seem to be bothered by the same possibility.

Of course she had known of her father's continuing friendship with the younger man; he occasionally talked of having seen or spoken to Falkner. Conversations that Skye had listened to avidly while at the same time maintaining an outward indifference, desperate that no one, least of all her father, should realize how deeply and irrevocably she had fallen in love with Falkner six years ago.

But even so, she wouldn't have thought, based on the things her father had said about the other man, that their friendship had been such that Falkner would now feel a responsibility to come to the aid of Connor's daughter.

But what other reason could he possibly have for being here…?

'Skye, Connor was there for me after the accident three years ago,' Falkner rasped. 'And again two years ago,' he added reluctantly.

Two years ago? What had happened two years… Ah.

She had read in the newspapers of Falkner's marriage five years ago, followed by his even more publicized separation after the accident, and the messy divorce that had followed a year later.

'Connor spent a lot of his valuable time two years ago talking to me, helping me come to terms with—things,' Falkner continued harshly.

And this was obviously Falkner's way of returning the older man's generosity.

Well, at least he was honest, Skye accepted ruefully. Even if it might have been more comforting, if unlikely, if his concern had been a little more personally directed.

She sighed, turning to look uninterestedly out at the passing countryside, recognizing some of it, aware that they would shortly be arriving at Falkner's home.

There was one positive thing to look forward to, at least: his wife wouldn't be there waiting to welcome her—or otherwise.

She had wondered, five years ago, what the woman was like when Falkner had married, the photograph of the two of them that had appeared in the newspapers at the time of their marriage not only grainy, making their features indistinct, but also in black and white.

Whatever Selina Harrington's personality and looks, the marriage had only lasted a rocky two years, Selina leaving Falkner shortly after his accident, divorcing him a year later amid claims of his involvement with another woman.

There was a thought. Maybe the 'other woman' would be at the Falkner home waiting to welcome her, instead.

Skye shifted uncomfortably in the cream leather seat. 'Er—I really don't want to put you or—or anyone else—' she chewed worriedly on her bottom lip '—to any inconvenience, by turning up at your house in this way.'

'You won't be,' Falkner told her with assured dismissal.

Not exactly a helpful reply; she already knew Falkner well enough to realize he was arrogant enough to expect that other people's reactions to his unexpected guest would be reflective of his own.

Whereas Skye had learnt only too well the last few months just how hurtful a cold rebuff could be. Goodness knew, there had been enough of them recently.

She drew in a deep breath. 'Falkner, what—?'

'Let's just get through the rest of this week, hmm?' he prompted abruptly. 'There will be plenty of time to—talk, later, okay?'

The rest of this week…

Her father's funeral.

Incredible.

Unbelievable.

When she still had the feeling he was going to walk through the door demanding a mug of the strong coffee that had kept him going through their long working day, or that she was going to turn a corner and he would be there waiting for her, as big and protective as he had always been, giving that big booming laugh that told her everything was right with the world.

What was she going to do without him?

The two of them had always been so close, more so since there had really only ever been the two of them.

Skye couldn't imagine her life without him in it. Didn't want to imagine a life without him!

She was suddenly overwhelmed by such a feeling of despair that she wasn't even aware of Falkner's sharp glance in her direction, or the fact that he pulled the car over into a lay-by, turning off the engine before releasing his seat belt and turning to take her into his arms.

It was the warmth of those arms, being cradled against the solid hardness of a human chest, that was Skye's complete undoing. The sob caught at the back of her throat, choking her, her body racked by those sobs as she gave into her feelings of complete desolation.

'It's all right, Skye,' Falkner murmured, his hands moving comfortingly up and down her spine as he held her close against him. 'I'm here. I'll be here for as long as you need me. Skye, don't…' he groaned with aching concern as his words only made her cry all the harder.

Seconds ago she had been overwhelmed by feelings of loneliness, emptiness, but as Falkner's words penetrated the pain that consumed her, the warmth of his arms protecting her, she knew she wasn't completely alone, that he meant what he said: he would be there for her for as long as she needed him.

But with that realization came the knowledge of the danger that awaited her there, a danger she had no idea, at this moment when she needed him so much, how to cope with; it would be all too easy to just let Falkner take over, to stay with him and never leave. And, loving him as she did, she knew she couldn't do that.

She pulled back slightly, brushing the tears from her cheeks with the back of her hand. 'I'm all right now,' she dismissed, not quite able to meet the penetration of his searching blue gaze. 'It was just—for a moment—

I'm all right now,' she repeated determinedly, pulling fully out of his arms to sit back against the door. As far away from Falkner as was possible in the close confines of the car.

'Sure?' he prompted gently.

She swallowed hard. If he was going to carry on being kind to her like this she knew she wouldn't be able to cope. 'Of course I'm sure,' she told him tartly. 'Let's go, Falkner,' she snapped as she sensed his continued gaze on her, her jaw clenched determinedly as she refused to return that gaze.

'Okay,' he finally accepted tersely, turning on the ignition to manoeuvre the car back into the flow of traffic. 'Skye, we're going to arrive in a few minutes, and—'

So there would be someone else there.

'Don't worry, Falkner,' she cut in coldly. 'I'll promise I'll try to be as unobtrusive as possible for the next couple of days. In fact, if you just show me to a bedroom, I can stay there until—until after Friday,' she continued determinedly. 'No one need even know I'm staying with you. You—'

'Skye—shut up,' he cut in harshly, his hands tightly gripping the steering wheel. 'I don't care who knows you're there. I don't care if you choose to walk around the house stark naked!' he added grimly. 'Am I making myself clear?'

'Very.' Her mouth twisted into the semblance of a smile at his obvious anger at her suggestion it might be better for him if he just hid her away somewhere. 'But I think I'll forgo the "walking around the house stark naked" bit, if you don't mind!'

'Pity.' He shrugged. 'It might have been—diverting,' he drawled. 'Although perhaps impractical with my housekeeper living in the house,' he dismissed briskly, turning the car down the long gravel driveway that led to his house.

His housekeeper…

Skye gave him a searching glance, her confusion such that she didn't know how to reply to his first statement. No doubt Falkner was just trying to divert her attention onto something less traumatic than the next couple of days—and no doubt he had succeeded.

The thought of her ever feeling confident enough around Falkner to stroll around his home naked was enough to confuse anyone!

'You were saying something about when we arrive?' she reminded him stiltedly.

'It doesn't matter,' he dismissed tersely as he parked the car outside the house. 'We can talk about that later too.'

There seemed to be an awful lot of things they were going to talk about later…?

But Skye put all that from her mind as Falkner got out of the car to come round and open her door for her, supporting her arm as she stepped down, nevertheless the movement causing pain to her ribs.

Falkner looked at her ruefully as she finally stood on the gravel driveway beside him. 'You look as if you've gone ten rounds with Lennox Lewis,' he drawled in answer to her questioning look.

She grimaced. 'Believe me, parts of me feel as if I've gone ten rounds with Lennox Lewis!'

Falkner laughed softly, his hand on her elbow as they walked up the stone steps to the front door.

Skye had noticed that the driveway and grounds looked cared for as they drove up, and the house no longer had that run-down look of six years ago, either;

obviously stocks and shares had proved more lucrative
for Falkner than showjumping!

She drew in a deep breath now as she prepared to face
what lay in store for her behind the huge oak door,
friend or foe, she had no idea.

'It will be all right, Skye,' Falkner told her firmly as
he seemed to read her uncertainty. 'I'm here, remember,'
he added determinedly.

Yes, he was. And she still had no real idea why he
should be. But he had promised to be 'here' for as long
as she needed him.

As long as it took her to get through this nightmare?

If she ever did!

'Feel like going for a walk outside?' Falkner
prompted once they had finished with the delicious afternoon tea brought in by his bustlingly friendly
Scottish housekeeper.

Within seconds of meeting the middle-aged woman
Skye had known she had nothing to fear where the
other woman was concerned; Annie Graham treated
Falkner like a rather naughty child, and within minutes
of their meeting had treated Skye in the same affectionately friendly way, urging her to eat some of the sandwiches and scones with the words 'you need some skin
on those bones'.

No doubt the older woman would have something to
say when she realized that neither of them had done
justice to the delicious tea, Skye acknowledged ruefully.

Maybe that was the reason for Falkner's suggestion
the two of them go for a walk? A walk that would cause
him more than a little discomfort.

'Or perhaps you would rather go upstairs and rest for

a while?' Falkner realized lightly. 'You've had a busy afternoon so far.'

Skye shook her head. 'I think I've rested enough this last week. But if you have something else you should be doing…?' After all, he had already spent enough of his day with her.

He stood up. 'Take a walk with me.' He held out his hand to help her stand up.

Skye shied away, from that hand, and the idea of going outside. Annie Graham had proved warm and welcoming, but that didn't mean she would get the same reception from other members of Falkner's household staff.

Falkner frowned darkly, still holding out his hand to her. 'Skye, no matter how much you might feel like doing so just now, you really can't just sit in here and hide from the world,' he rasped.

She glared up at him. 'Who says I can't?' she challenged resentfully.

'I do,' he replied without hesitation. 'You know as well as I do, Skye, that when you've been thrown from a horse, you have to get straight back up into the saddle.'

'Is that what you did—?' She broke off with a gasp as she realized how insensitive she was being; of course that wasn't what he had done, his injuries had been such that he probably couldn't ride at all any more. 'This isn't the same,' she muttered awkwardly.

'It is.' Falkner nodded abruptly. 'And your father would tell you exactly the same—'

'Don't presume to tell me what my father would or wouldn't say!' Her eyes glittered furiously.

He gave an impatient sigh. 'Skye, you're only angry because you know I'm right,' he rasped.

Yes, she was; her father had always been a pragmatic

man. His philosophy had always been, if you fell or received a knock of some kind, then you picked yourself up and carried on. It was what he had done after Skye's mother died. During the last difficult six months, too. It was what he would want Skye to do now…

She knew that as well as Falkner obviously did.

But none of that changed the fact that just the thought of going with Falkner, of walking outside with him, where someone might recognize her, made Skye squirm with discomfort.

'I'm feeling rather tired, Falkner—'

'Coward,' he murmured softly.

But not so softly that Skye couldn't hear him. Or resent him for being right.

She was behaving like a coward, and her father would have been disappointed in her, would have launched into some lengthy Irish parable that made a mockery of her fear.

But, she realized impatiently, Falkner's method of making her angry had exactly the same effect.

'Okay!' she agreed forcefully, ignoring the hand he held out to her, ignoring the pain in her ribs as she struggled to her feet without help. 'Satisfied?' she added challengingly, blue eyes sparkling with resentment.

'Perfectly,' Falkner answered lightly, opening the door for her to precede him.

Skye did so stiffly. And not just because of her painful ribs; she really didn't want to do this.

'Okay?' Falkner prompted softly a few minutes later as they approached the stables. It was curiously quiet, none of the bustle of activity here today that there had been six years ago.

'Okay,' she echoed tensely.

'This way.' He turned to the left, leading her down the long row of closed individual stables, his limp more noticeable now. .

'I don't understand, Falkner; where are we going?' Skye frowned her puzzlement as she followed reluctantly.

Why on earth was he taking her round his deserted stables? Perhaps this was Falkner's version of that 'Irish parable' her father would have subjected her to, something along the lines of 'he had succeeded despite no longer being involved in his love of showjumping', as she would have to survive without her beloved father. If that was what this was about, then Falkner was wasting his time, because she—

'Almost there,' he dismissed lightly—that lightness belied by the heavy frown between his brows.

'I—' Skye broke off as she heard a familiar sound, her whole body tensing as she turned in the direction of that sound, and she realized not all of the stables were empty after all, eyes widening in shocked surprise as that whinny of recognition was loudly repeated. 'Storm…?' she questioned dazedly, hurrying to the open stable door several stalls down, staring in total disbelief as the massive head stretched across the top of the open door to nuzzle ecstatically against her face. 'Storm!' she acknowledged chokingly, burying her own face into his glistening black neck, tears falling hotly down her cheeks as her arms clung to him weakly.

It had been the shock of her young life six years ago when, three months after her initial meeting with Falkner, a horsebox had arrived late one evening at her father's stable, the door opening to reveal a very disgruntled Storm.

Skye had turned to her father dazedly as she'd easily recognized the horse.

'Falkner changed his mind,' her father told her with satisfaction. 'He telephoned me one day last week and offered to let me buy Storm, after all.' He shrugged. 'I didn't tell you because I wanted it to be a total surprise for you,' he added happily.

A total surprise had to be an understatement. Falkner Harrington hadn't looked like a man who ever changed his mind about anything, and after the blistering rebuke he had given her three months earlier, once she had walked back to his house, Skye had been sure he would never allow her so much as near one of his horses again, let alone allow her to own one.

But there Storm was, as big and beautiful as ever. And—miraculously—he was hers.

'This is literally a case of "never look a gift horse in the mouth", me darlin',' her father teased as he slipped his arm about her shoulders, giving her a hug as they both looked admiringly at the prancing stallion.

That was how Skye had come to own Storm, after all—but it certainly didn't explain what Storm was doing back in England now.

He should still be in Ireland, at her father's stable, had certainly been there a week ago when they'd last spoken to Uncle Seamus on the telephone.

She turned to look at Falkner, her arms still wrapped around Storm's neck, the paleness of her face showing the tracks of her tears. 'Why—how—when—?' She gave a helpless shrug, totally overwhelmed by this latest development.

'I brought him back from Ireland with me last night,' Falkner told her evenly. 'Although he certainly wasn't as sweet-tempered as this on the journey,' he added ruefully.

No, she could imagine he hadn't been. Storm hated

travel of any sort, part of that 'temperament' Falkner had once referred to, and crossing the Irish Sea in a horsebox must have seemed like the ultimate in discomfort to him.

Falkner's explanation told Skye 'how' and 'when', but it still didn't explain 'why'…

Storm hadn't left Ireland since the day he'd been delivered to her six years ago, had made his feelings clear from the beginning concerning even the possibility of being put into a horsebox again, let alone being taken anywhere in one.

Yet Falkner had somehow managed to bring the horse back from Ireland with him yesterday, something that must have been as uncomfortable for him, with his injured leg, as it must have been to the horse…

Skye shook her head. She didn't understand any of this. Friday, the day of her father's funeral, was going to be the second worst day in her life—the day her father died would always be the worst—but surely after that there would be no further need for her to remain in England.

And yet Falkner said he had brought the horse back from Ireland with him only yesterday—

'What were you doing in Ireland?' she questioned sharply.

Falkner grimaced admiringly. 'That bump on the head hasn't slowed you down any, has it?'

'I was suffering from concussion, Falkner, not brain damage,' she returned dismissively.

He shrugged. 'I had no idea what had happened to— didn't know about the accident,' he bit out flatly, 'until I saw that awful photograph of you in the newspaper—'

'I'm surprised you recognized me,' Skye derided.

Falkner gave an acknowledging inclination of his

head. 'It wasn't easy,' he conceded dryly. 'You're looking a lot better now,' he added encouragingly.

'Really?' she speculated. 'Then I must have looked
pretty awful earlier in the week.' She had looked a
complete wreck when she'd glanced at herself in the
mirror at the hospital earlier.

'You did,' Falkner confirmed bluntly. 'You were also,
according to the officious ward receptionist when I telephoned, refusing all visitors. I was given the distinct impression that wasn't negotiable, so, rather than kick my
heels waiting for you to be well enough to be discharged, I flew over to Ireland to see if there was
anything I could do there instead.' He sighed. 'Your
uncle Seamus is a self-pitying drunk,' he stated flatly.

'Yes,' she confirmed heavily; there was no doubting that
he had become so since his wife had left him a year ago.

Falkner shrugged. 'The housekeeper is quite happy
to stay on, and I talked to your father's groom, and he's
quite prepared to take care of the horses, but I thought
you might rather have Storm here with you.'

Which explanation still left the question mark—
why bring Storm here at all when the likelihood was
that she would be returning to Ireland herself in another
week or so?

Wouldn't she…?

CHAPTER THREE

'I WOULD suggest you have an early night, Skye,' Falkner murmured after dinner. 'You've had a very busy day,' he added gently as she looked up at him dazedly.

Yes, she accepted it had been busy after her recent days of inertia, she just wasn't sure going to bed early was such a good idea. It would give her longer to lay awake. Thinking.

Besides, she wasn't in the least tired, still had far too many questions left unanswered to possibly be able to sleep. But Falkner had been more than usually uncommunicative as the two of them had eaten dinner together—a dinner neither of them had done justice to— and Skye could appreciate that Falkner probably had things of his own he wanted to deal with now. Maybe friends—or a particular friend—he would like to call…?

'I'm sure you must have lots of things to do, Falkner. Please don't let me keep you from them,' Skye assured him. 'I'm just not tired yet.' After all, it was only nine-thirty. 'Please don't worry about me,' she dismissed lightly as he continued to frown.

'But I do worry about you, Skye,' he drawled.

She shook her head. 'There really is no need, and it's

far too early for me to go to bed yet.' And actually stand any chance of sleeping.

'In that case…do you play chess?' He raised dark brows.

Her eyes narrowed. 'Badly.'

'Hmm.' He grimaced. 'Then how about—?'

'Falkner, I am not a child in need of entertainment,' she assured him impatiently as she stood up, ignoring the painful twinges in her side as she did so; whatever the pain, she had really had enough of Falkner towering over her in this way.

His expression darkened. 'Maybe all this would be easier if you were still a child!' he snapped harshly.

Skye frowned her puzzlement at his harshness. 'I don't know what you mean…?'

'No,' he sighed, 'I don't suppose you do.' He shook his head. 'Skye, I'm doing my best, in very unusual circumstances, so maybe you could just cut me a little slack, okay?' His eyes glittered challengingly.

Considering the man she had briefly known six years ago, Skye knew that he was more than doing his best where she was concerned. And she accepted they were unusual circumstances. It was just—Skye felt so angry. With herself. With Falkner. With Uncle Seamus. With— of all people—her father. How could she possibly feel angry with her beloved father? It wasn't his fault that he—that he—

She pushed that thought very firmly from her mind, her face pale with the effort. 'Falkner, why did you bother going to the trouble of bringing Storm over here?' He had neatly avoided answering that question when they had left the stables earlier, lingering to have a lengthy conversation with one of the gardeners, and there had been little chance to introduce the subject again since that time. Well, blow politeness. She wanted an answer. And she wanted it now.

He thrust his hands into the pockets of his tailored trousers, having changed before they had dinner. 'I thought you would like him to be here when you came out of hospital. A friendly face, so to speak,' he added ruefully.

Skye's mouth quirked humourlessly. 'You didn't think yours would be enough on its own?'

Falkner looked a little less grim as he grimaced derisively. 'I haven't had that impression so far in our acquaintance, no!' he returned dryly.

Skye's eyes widened incredulously. Did he really not know—? Could he not see—?

Obviously not, she realized with relief; everything was awful enough already, without having Falkner feeling sorry for her because she'd had the misfortune to fall in love with him six years ago—and remained that way.

She drew in a deep breath. 'I'm sorry if I've given the impression I'm less than grateful for what you're doing.'

Falkner laughed softly. 'Skye, I can assure you I never expected you to run joyfully into my arms.'

He would never know the temptation she had had to do exactly that when he'd arrived in her hospital room earlier today. If her painful ribs hadn't prevented it. If her own pride hadn't forbidden it. If she hadn't lain in that bed willing herself not to show him exactly how pleased she was to see him.

Falkner was both the first—and last—person she needed to be kind to her just now.

She shook her head. 'I doubt I could run anywhere at this moment,' she avoided. 'Falkner, I—I'm very appreciative of all you've done for me—'

'You sound like a little girl about to refuse a birthday party invitation!' he derided.

Her eyes sparkled angrily. 'You aren't making this easy for me, either,' she protested impatiently.

'Maybe when you stop apologizing for your very existence, I might just do that. But until that time...' He shrugged.

'You'll just keep irritating me,' she guessed heavily.

His eyes widened. 'Is that what I'm doing? Maybe I'm just wondering where the Skye O'Hara is that jumped on Storm's back six years ago and rode off into the sunset.'

Her cheeks felt warm at this reminder of her earlier impetuosity. 'I grew up?'

Falkner's gaze travelled slowly over her from head to toe, from the short-cropped hair, the thinness of her elfin features, to the almost boyish slenderness of her body.

Skye shifted uncomfortably under the lengthiness of that probing gaze. Why didn't he say something? Anything!

'So you did,' he finally murmured huskily. 'And very nicely too.'

Her eyes widened. 'I beg your pardon?'

His mouth twisted humourlessly. 'I'm sure you heard me the first time—but I'll repeat it if you would like—'

'No! No,' she repeated more calmly, wondering how the conversation had suddenly become so—so intimate. When intimacy was the last thing she had ever expected from Falkner.

'What's the matter, Skye?' Falkner was suddenly standing much closer than was comfortable. 'Issuing challenges you have no intention of honouring?'

Her eyes flashed warningly. 'I can meet any challenge you care to make!'

'Really?' He really was too close now, so close Skye could feel the warmth of his body, the warmth of his breath stirring the tendrils of hair at her temple. 'Let's see, shall we…?' He swept Skye into his arms, his mouth coming down forcefully on hers.

She had been waiting for this all her life, it seemed, had longed for the feel of Falkner's lips moving so erotically against hers, the strength of his arms about her, giving herself up to the sheer pleasure of being close to him.

With a murmur of capitulation her body moulded to each hard contour of Falkner's, her arms moving up about his neck as she returned his kiss with all the longing she had held in check for so long.

Falkner groaned low in his throat as his hands moved restlessly down her spine and over the slenderness of her hips, pulling her fiercely into the hardness of his body, his arousal more than evident.

And all the time his mouth continued that pleasurable assault on hers, his tongue moving searchingly over the moistness of her lips before exploring deeper.

Skye no longer had any idea where Falkner began and she ended, just wanting him to go on making love to her, to—

'No!' Falkner ended their lovemaking so suddenly that Skye swayed unsteadily on her feet as he placed her firmly away from him, a nerve pulsing in his tightly clenched jaw as he looked at her with glittering blue eyes. 'This is not a good idea, Skye,' he rasped harshly. 'You have no idea what you're doing,' he added self-disgustedly.

She was kissing the man she loved, the man she had longed to hold her for the last six years.

'I had no right to do that,' he continued gruffly. 'I— I apologize.'

He 'apologized'. For kissing her, for making love to her. Tears flooded her eyes now as she looked at him dazedly.

'You were right earlier, Skye,' he added harshly. 'I do have things to do.' He turned on his heel, walking briskly over to the door. 'I suppose it's useless for me to ask you to take things easy for a day or two?' he paused to add impatiently. Skye could have no idea how forlorn a figure she looked standing alone in the middle of the gracious elegance of Falkner's lounge—but she could take a pretty good guess! She was visibly physically battered and bruised, and as for emotionally—!

'You can ask,' she allowed heavily.

'That's what I thought,' he snapped irritably. 'I accept that you'll probably want to spend time with Storm, just don't attempt riding him just yet, hmm? This time I might be tempted into giving you the warmed backside I should have given you six years ago.' He closed the door forcefully behind him.

Instead of which he had kissed her until she was almost senseless.

And he had just done it again....

The tears felt hot on her cheeks, and she dashed them away impatiently; she had done nothing but cry since Falkner had collected her from the hospital, it seemed.

Would this nightmare ever end?

'I thought you would still be upstairs asleep in bed.' Falkner came to an abrupt halt in the kitchen doorway as he saw Skye seated at the table placed at one end of the cosily large room.

Skye gave a guilty start of surprise at his sudden entrance; at five-thirty in the morning she hadn't thought anyone else would be awake. The silence in the house when she'd come quietly down the stairs half an hour ago had seemed to indicate as much.

But Falkner was already dressed in a casual blue shirt and faded denims, his hair damp from the shower.

Unlike Skye, who hadn't bothered to dress before coming downstairs, still wearing the short cotton nightshirt she wore to sleep in. Except she hadn't slept...

She sat back now, giving a shrug. 'I couldn't sleep. I hope you don't mind, but I thought coming down here and having a hot drink might help.' She grimaced at the mug of coffee in front of her.

Although it was already daylight outside, it was gloomy in the kitchen, the single light from above the cooker the only illumination in the room, throwing Falkner's features into grim relief. He looked less than pleased to see her here.

He drew in a harsh breath, nodding abruptly before coming further into the room. 'It doesn't seem to have worked,' he murmured dryly.

Well, it might have done—if Falkner hadn't just walked in. But, as usual, she found his presence disturbing, feeling even less sleepy now than she had an hour ago.

'No,' she conceded huskily. 'Er—there's coffee in the pot if you're interested,' she invited.

Ordinarily she would have got up and poured it for him, but, as her nightshirt only reached just below her bare thighs, she didn't feel inclined to move at the moment. In fact, she felt altogether underdressed to be in Falkner's company at all.

'Didn't you make rather a lot of coffee for just "a hot drink"?' Falkner pointedly eyed the half full coffee-pot as he poured himself a cup.

She swallowed hard. 'I didn't think—I always

make—made, a huge pot of coffee every morning for my father when we were at home. I just did it automatically. Da always said I made good coffee,' she concluded lamely, her cheeks pale as she realized exactly what she had done. Everything she said and did reminded her of her beloved father.

Nothing was ever going to be the same. If this all felt like a nightmare, what on earth was it going to be like when she went back to Ireland, with no Da to care for, or Da to care for her?

'He was right,' Falkner murmured as he moved to sit opposite her at the kitchen table. 'You do make good coffee.' He took another appreciative sip.

This was all so strange, sitting here in the early hours of the morning in her skimpy nightshirt, talking to Falkner of all people. If she had ever thought of seeing him again—and she would be lying if she said she hadn't thought of that a lot during the last six years!— it certainly hadn't been under these circumstances.

She had always imagined herself as that sophisticated beauty she had wished herself to be six years ago, of bowling Falkner over with that beauty, so much so that he couldn't help but fall in love with her in return.

Instead of which she looked, as he had already said, as if she had been in a fight—and lost.

'What are you doing up so early?' she prompted lightly.

Falkner grimaced. 'I couldn't sleep, either.'

She frowned. 'Nothing to do with me, I hope?'

His eyes narrowed in the gloom. 'Why should you think it might have anything to do with you?' he rasped.

Skye was taken aback at his harshness. 'I only meant—thought—'

'I do have other concerns in my life besides you, you

know, Skye,' he continued with cold dismissal, placing his empty cup down on the table with a controlled thud.

Of course he did. She knew that he did. Until this past week, when he had once again been thrust into awareness of her existence, he probably hadn't given her a thought for the last six years.

'I'm sorry—'

'I'm sorry—'

'After you,' Falkner invited wearily as they both began talking at the same time.

She shook her head. 'I'm really sorry you've become involved in all this, Falkner.'

'All what?' he prompted softly.

'I—the accident. My being here. All of it!' She couldn't go on any more.

He made an impatient movement of dismissal. 'It was my choice to become involved, Skye.'

'But—'

'No buts,' he cut in firmly. 'I'm sorry, I shouldn't have snapped at you just now,' he added self-disgustedly.

Skye gave a grimace. 'Falkner, this whole—situation, is going to become even more ridiculous if we feel the need to apologize to each other for everything we say over the next four days.'

'Four days?' he echoed frowningly.

Skye avoided his probing gaze now. 'Until after—once the funeral is over—'

'Skye, I don't think you should consider going back to Ireland for a few weeks, at least,' he cut in firmly. 'For one thing you aren't fit enough to travel anywhere yet. For another—' He broke off, his expression guarded, it seemed to Skye. 'I—there's nothing there for you, Skye,' he finally added determinedly.

Skye flinched at the truth of his words. All that remained of her life in Ireland was an empty house. Even Storm was now comfortably stabled here.

She had realized the previous evening, after Falkner had walked off, that once again he hadn't exactly answered her question as to why he had brought Storm here, but perhaps he just had…

'There's Uncle Seamus,' she reminded sharply.

If anything Falkner's expression became even more determined. 'I believe I've already made my opinion of your uncle Seamus more than clear.'

'Yes, you have,' she sighed, remembering that opinion only too well. 'But he's had a tough time this last year—'

'And you haven't?' Falkner reasoned harshly.

She shrugged. 'My wife didn't walk out on me after five years of marriage.'

'Frankly, Skye, having now met your uncle Seamus, I'm surprised it took her that long!' Falkner's tone was scathing.

If Skye were truthful, so was she. Uncle Seamus had met and married Aunt Shanna in Dublin more than five years ago, the two of them enjoying the hectic social life there, Uncle Seamus's decision to move to the family's country estate two years ago not suiting Aunt Shanna at all. A year ago she had announced that she couldn't stand living in the country a moment longer, and had moved back to Dublin. Which was when Uncle Seamus's drinking bouts had become even heavier than usual.

But she didn't exactly welcome Falkner's open criticism of her uncle.

'At least he only drank his marriage away,' she defended heatedly.

And just as instantly regretted it as she saw the ominous way Falkner's face darkened. With good reason, she accepted uncomfortably; she had no idea of the circumstances behind his own marriage breakdown, had only read in the newspapers the things his wife had accused him of.

Falkner had become dangerously still. 'Meaning what exactly?' he prompted softly.

But Skye wasn't in the least fooled by the mildness of his tone, knew that she had touched a raw nerve. One she had no right expressing an opinion on.

She closed her eyes briefly before once again looking across the table at him. 'Falkner, I didn't mean—'

'Yes, you did, damn it,' he rasped, pushing the chair back to get noisily to his feet. 'You know nothing about my marriage, Skye, or the reasons for its breakdown. Nothing,' he repeated harshly, his eyes seeming to glitter silver in the subdued lighting as he glared down at her.

Lighting Skye was grateful for as she felt her cheeks pale. 'You're right, I don't.' She swallowed hard. 'I was just—I shouldn't have—'

'Forget it,' he rasped, shaking his head with impatient dismissal.

'I have a meeting in London this morning,' he added abruptly. 'Do you think you can you manage to amuse yourself for a few hours?'

He was being deliberately insulting now, Skye recognized, at the same time acknowledging that he had a perfect right to be after what she had just implied about the breakdown of his marriage, and subsequent divorce.

'Yes,' she confirmed huskily, looking down at the table so that she no longer had to see the anger in his face.

Or watch him leave.

Because she suddenly felt bereft at the thought of him going. Oh, she knew Mrs Graham would be in the house somewhere for the morning, so she wouldn't be alone, but that wasn't the same as having Falkner here…

'Skye…?'

She couldn't look up, knew that he would see the tears in her eyes if she did that. 'Don't let me keep you, Falkner,' she dismissed hardly.

'I—Skye, are you crying?' he demanded impatiently, coming down on his haunches beside her chair to put his hand under her chin so that he could look into her face. 'You are crying,' he realized exasperatedly even as he pulled her roughly into his arms, cradling her head against his shoulder.

The tears felt like hot lava falling down her cheeks, and they wouldn't stop falling, the shoulder of Falkner's shirt soaking wet with them by the time Skye raised her head to look at him.

'I can't believe this.' She shook her head emotionally. 'I hadn't cried at all until—until you came to the hospital yesterday.' And now she couldn't stop.

'Then it's past time that you did,' Falkner said grimly.

Perhaps. But she didn't like breaking down like this in front of Falkner. 'I've made your shirt all wet—'

'I have plenty of others I can change into,' he dismissed impatiently, his gaze searching on the paleness of her face. 'Skye, do you want to come with me?'

She blinked. 'To London?'

His expression softened slightly. 'It isn't quite the den of iniquity it's cracked up to be—especially at nine o'clock in the morning!'

Skye grimaced. 'I know that. I just thought—won't I be in the way?'

'Possibly,' he answered with his usual bluntness. 'But I can live with that.'

Skye gave a watery smile. 'In that case, I'll stay here.' Contrarily, it was the fact that he had said she could go with him that was enough for her to know she would be okay here until his return, after all.

Falkner raised his eyes heavenwards. 'Women! Or rather—woman!' he corrected dryly. 'I don't think I'll ever understand any of you!'

'Would you want to?' Skye mused ruefully. 'I thought it was those unexplainable differences between men and women that made us interesting to each other?'

Falkner put her firmly back on her chair before straightening, wincing slightly as he straightened his right leg. 'Maybe,' he accepted dryly. 'It's too early in the morning for me to be able to figure that one out!'

Skye frowned as he stepped awkwardly away from her, noticing that he put most of his weight on his left leg as he did so, moistening her lips before speaking. 'Does it—does your leg still hurt you?'

It was as if a shutter had come down over those expressive blue eyes, his expression once again remotely distant. 'Yes, it still hurts me,' he rasped evenly. 'Why do you want to know?' he snapped harshly.

She frowned. 'I just wondered—' She broke off, realizing she was overstepping a line as she saw the way his jaw had tightened ominously.

'Yes?' Falkner prompted tautly. 'You just wondered what?' he pressured as she chewed uncomfortably on her bottom lip.

She grimaced. 'If you can still ride. And if—if you missed competing professionally,' she admitted regretfully, wishing she had never started this conversation.

He drew himself up to his full impressive height, towering over her now. 'Not that it's any of your business—but, yes, I can still ride,' he bit out coldly. 'After a fashion. As for competing…' His expression became bleak. 'I would have had to give that up one day, anyway.'

Yes, but not in the abrupt way he had been forced to do so. He had been, and had remained so until the day of his accident, one of the top riders in the world; surely he had to miss all that?

'Skye,' he snapped as he seemed to read the sympathy in her eyes—and deeply resented it! 'You should already know that self-pity is an emotion I have no time for,' he harshly reminded her of his remarks of yesterday. 'As for other people's sympathy—! I would suggest that you concentrate on your own injuries, and leave me to concentrate on mine!' he rasped scathingly before turning away. 'I should be back by lunchtime, but if I'm not, go ahead and eat without me.'

As she watched him limp over towards the door Skye wondered if she would ever feel like eating again.

She hadn't meant to upset him; goodness knew, he had been nothing but kind to her, in his own unique way, since coming to the hospital yesterday. She just couldn't help her feelings of curiosity concerning him, wanted to know everything that had happened to him in the six years since she had last seen him. And beyond.

'And, Skye…' He paused to turn as he reached the open kitchen door.

She looked across at him hopefully. 'Yes?'

His mouth twisted derisively. 'I know I originally said I didn't mind if you walked around my home stark naked, but if you feel the need to come downstairs again for a drink in the middle of the night, put some more

clothes on, hmm? Mrs Graham might be shocked!'
came his parting shot before he left the kitchen, quietly
closing the door behind him.

Skye stared after him open-mouthed. She hadn't
thought—hadn't given any thought—Falkner must have
been able to feel her nakedness beneath the nightshirt
as he'd held her in his arms a few minutes ago.

And why not? Hadn't she been as aware of him with
every inch of her being…?

CHAPTER FOUR

'EXACTLY what do you think you're doing?'

Skye gave a guilty start as she recognized the harshness of Falkner's voice, straightening slowly to look over Storm's withers to where Falkner stood at the stable door, his expression unreadable with the sunlight filtering into the stable from behind him. But the impatience in his voice was enough of an indication of his mood.

'Grooming Storm?' she answered unnecessarily; it must be perfectly obvious what she was doing.

'Against the doctor's instructions,' he rebuked harshly. 'Against my instructions,' he added irritably as he came into the stable, locking the lower door behind him as he did so.

Skye had a pretty good idea which of those instructions Falkner considered the more important.

But she had spent most of the morning in the cosiness of the kitchen talking to Mrs Graham or flicking through one of the cookery books that were all the reading matter the other woman had. She'd eaten the light lunch of scrambled eggs the housekeeper had insisted on preparing for her, and still Falkner hadn't returned from his business meeting. Left with a choice between making a nuisance of herself in the kitchen all afternoon, or coming out to the stable to see Storm, Skye had known exactly which one she preferred to do.

It had seemed silly once she was in the stable not to give Storm a soothing groom... Although she could see by Falkner's disapproving expression as he stepped into the light that he didn't quite see it that way.

'I'm fine, Falkner,' she assured him lightly, giving Storm another brush to prove her point. 'See. It doesn't hurt a bit.'

Falkner looked as if he was having great difficulty not giving her that 'warmed backside' he had mentioned yesterday! 'I leave you alone for a few hours—'

'Falkner, I'm twenty-four years old, not four!' Her eyes flashed a warning at him across Storm's withers.

He looked at her scathingly. 'A four-year-old with broken ribs would have known not to groom a horse. You just can't be trusted to behave yourself even for a few hours, can you?'

Skye became very still. 'I can be trusted, Falkner,' she assured him, her jaw clenched in an effort not to completely lose her temper.

'I disagree—I didn't mean in that way, Skye,' he bit out exasperatedly as he suddenly realized what she meant. 'I have never believed those stories about Connor,' he said quietly.

So many other people had though, the collapse of O'Hara Whiskey still under investigation. But there was little point to that now, Skye acknowledged bitterly; with her father dead, what difference did it make why or how the company had failed in the way that it had...?

'Skye?'

She looked across at Falkner, mentally shaking her-

self out of her despondency. 'Did you have a successful morning?' she prompted lightly.

He shrugged, his hands thrust deep into his
pockets. 'Not bad,' he dismissed enigmatically. 'I
won't bother to ask what you did with your morning,'
he added reprovingly.

Letting her know she wasn't going to get off that
lightly!

'I thought I was a guest here, Falkner,' she snapped,
'not a prisoner!'

His face darkened at the accusation. 'And I thought
you were convalescing after your recent injuries!'

'I am,' she sighed, moving to put the grooming equip-
ment back in its box. 'But I'm bored, Falkner,' she
groaned. 'There's only so many recipe books I can look
through without wanting to throw them out the window.
Especially as I can't cook.' She grimaced.

He raised blond brows. 'Not at all?'

She shrugged. 'Eggs and bacon, for when we had
early starts, but other than that, no, I can't cook,' she
admitted reluctantly; the next thing she knew, Falkner
would be insisting she spend time in the kitchen with
Mrs Graham taking cookery lessons! 'I was my father's
assistant, Falkner,' she added defensively. 'I can
organise an office, run a stable, make great coffee,' she
added pointedly. 'Even change a punctured tyre on any
vehicle you care to name, but any of the more feminine
accomplishments are beyond me.'

They had always had a housekeeper to run the house
in Ireland, and until Aunt Shanna's appearance in their
lives Skye hadn't even possessed a skirt or a dress, her
new aunt the one to insist on taking her shopping for
more feminine clothes.

Perhaps to some people her unbringing, until six years ago, by two old bachelors had been unorthodox, but Skye had certainly never felt as if she were missing out on anything.

Falkner smiled as she looked at him challengingly. 'In that case, you're going to make some lucky man a wonderful husband.'

She gave a disgusted snort. 'I'm not going to make some "lucky man" anything. I never intend to marry,' she told Falkner flatly as he looked at her questioningly.

He looked surprised. 'Why on earth not?'

'Because—' She broke off as Storm nuzzled her in protest of her distracted attention. 'He wants some exercise,' she told Falkner ruefully.

He nodded. 'I'll have George take him out. Give it a few days before you even attempt it yourself, Skye, hmm?' he prompted as her expression became wistful.

'Storm doesn't like anyone to ride him nowadays but me,' she protested.

'And me,' Falkner told her quietly. 'I rode him while I was in Ireland, Skye,' he explained as she looked at him sharply.

'You did…?' She couldn't hide her surprise at this; as Storm had got older, his temperament had become even more cantankerous, so much so that even their groom refused to ride him any more.

'He had to get used to me in a hurry if we were going to travel over here together,' Falkner told her briskly. 'As it was, he almost kicked in the side of the horsebox in an effort to show his displeasure!'

Skye turned back to the stallion. 'Poor darlin',' she crooned, her hand soothing on his glossy neck.

'And what about me?' Falkner prompted dryly.

She turned back to him, brows raised. 'You were there by choice—Storm wasn't!'

'Ungrateful little minx!' Falkner complained ruefully. 'I ached all over by the time we arrived back here at midnight.'

'I'm sure a hot bath soon sorted that out for you,' Skye came back dismissively.

Although she wasn't really as unsympathetic as she sounded, she just knew that Falkner wouldn't thank her for drawing attention to the injuries that obviously still caused him so much discomfort. But she had noticed that he was limping more heavily this afternoon, the drive and his time in London obviously having tired him more than he cared to admit, knew that the trip from Ireland with Storm must have been excruciatingly uncomfortable for him. Making her wonder once again why he had bothered...

'I can see I'm not going to get any sympathy from you,' Falkner muttered wryly. 'I'm driving into the town in a few minutes. Is there anything you need while I'm there?'

Skye's expression brightened. 'To go with you!'

He frowned. 'I don't think that's a good idea—'

'Why on earth not?' she protested.

'You're supposed to be resting—'

'If I rest much more today I'm going to scream!' she warned him determinedly.

Falkner sighed his impatience. 'And if I had known you were going to be this much trouble I would have left you in the hospital a few more days!'

Skye faced him defiantly in the confines of the stable. 'If I had known I was to be kept a prisoner here, I would have stayed there!'

He winced. 'That's the second time in the last few minutes that you've mentioned feeling like a prisoner. Is that really how you feel?'

Her shoulders sagged slightly as she realized how ungrateful she must sound. After all, at least Falkner had come to see her in hospital, which was more than could be said of any of her father's other so-called friends. The fact that Falkner had other things to do, which left her at rather a loose end, wasn't his fault.

'Not really,' she sighed heavily. 'I'm just—I think the phrase is "going stir crazy"!'

Falkner continued to look at her for several more long minutes before giving a slow nod of his head. 'Okay.'

Skye's eyes widened. 'Okay…?'

He nodded, eyes glittering teasingly. 'Okay.'

'I really can come with you?'

'You really can come with me,' he echoed dryly.

'Oh, Falkner, thank you, thank you!' She launched herself into his arms, immediately gasping with pain as two of her ribs reminded her they had recently been broken. 'Ouch!' she groaned self-derisively.

Although she made no effort to move away from Falkner. It felt so good to be there, so warm, so protective, so—so right, that she allowed herself the luxury for several more wonderful minutes.

His arms moved up slowly to wrap gently about her waist, his head coming down to rest on top of her as she snuggled against his shoulder.

Skye closed her eyes, knowing this was exactly where she had longed to be again for six long years. Of course, a lot had happened in those six years, to both of them, but at this precise moment, breathing in Falkner's sensual warmth, pressed close against the hardness of his body, Skye allowed herself to become lost in the sheer pleasure of just being there.

'Skye, I—hey!' Falkner snapped, moving back abruptly to turn and glare at Storm, the huge stallion looking down his long aristocratic nose at him in return. 'He bit me!' Falkner complained in surprise, releasing Skye to rub the shoulder the stallion had just taken a nip at.

Looking at the man and horse, glaring at each other in such similar ways, Skye couldn't hold back the laughter. In fact, she laughed so long and so hard that there were tears in her eyes when she at last straightened to look at them both.

Only to burst out laughing once again as she found both of them looking at her with questioning disdain.

'Now I know the reason you're never going to marry,' Falkner muttered as he took her arm to guide her out of the stable, locking the door firmly behind him, only for Storm's massive head to come out over the top in an attempt to take another nip at him. 'That monster won't let any man near you!' Falkner glared at the stallion as he sidestepped awkwardly.

Skye grinned. 'He doesn't argue with me, either.'

'He doesn't need to,' Falkner muttered, still massaging the shoulder Storm had taken a bite at.

Skye sobered, looking at him concernedly. 'Has he really hurt you? Perhaps I should take a look—'

'No,' Falkner rasped harshly, sighing as he saw the way her eyes widened in surprise at his vehemence. 'I'll be fine,' he dismissed. 'Let's get into town before all the shops close, shall we?' he added briskly.

Skye was quite happy with that suggestion. Although she couldn't help wondering why Falkner was so determined not to let her see his shoulder. She had read everything in the newspapers three years ago that she could find about his accident, had thought it was only his legs that were badly crushed, but maybe he had sustained other injuries that made him now rebuff her offer of help…?

'Would you like me to drive?' she offered as they reached the Range Rover parked on the driveway.

Falkner raised dark brows. 'Do you think you could?'

Probably not; although she would never admit it, her ribs ached very badly now. But Falkner looked so tired… 'I could have a go,' she offered.

'No, thanks.' He grimaced, opening the passenger door to help her up into the seat, losing his balance slightly as he did so. 'We look like a couple of old crocks!' he muttered once he was seated next to her behind the wheel.

'Speak for yourself!' Skye came back dryly.

Falkner turned the key in the ignition and put the vehicle in gear before looking at her derisively. 'You consider yourself still something of a baby, hmm?'

'I don't think of myself as either old or a crock, that's for certain,' she returned tartly.

Falkner shrugged. 'I can assure you that the injuries to my leg are of no consequence when I'm lying horizontal!'

Skye opened her mouth to give him another smart reply, instantly closing it again as she began to consider under what circumstances he would be lying horizontal.

'Well, well, speechless at last,' Falkner drawled mockingly as he drove the Range Rover down the gravel driveway and out onto the narrow lane.

For good reason! She had just had the most graphic picture inside her head of Falkner stark naked in a bed— lying horizontal. She didn't even want to think about the woman who might be lying beside him!

'Don't get too used to it,' she finally told him abruptly. 'I'm never at a loss for words for long.'

'So I've noticed,' he teased.

For all that brief exchange had thrown her into confusion, the silence that followed was companionable rather than awkward, Skye just enjoying being out in the fresh air. Alone with Falkner like this, surrounded by beautiful countryside, she could even forget for a few moments the nightmare her life had become...

The nearest town, as Falkner had called it, turned out to be a rather pretty country village that had grown into a market town over the years, its narrow streets and thatched cottages reminding Skye very much of home.

'I just need to get a few things from the chemist,' Skye told Falkner once he had parked the Range Rover in the square.

'I'll come with you,' he instantly offered.

'I—er—I would rather you didn't,' she refused awkwardly. 'I have some personal things to buy,' she added, face red with embarrassment; it was because those things were personal that she had come out at all!

'Personal—? Oh.' He paused, pursing his lips. 'Okay.' He finally nodded. 'I have to get some stamps from the post office, so we'll meet back here in a few minutes, if that's okay with you?'

It was more than okay. This was the first time for weeks, it seemed to Skye, that she had been on her own, with enough space to breathe in the peace she so desperately needed.

It was such a pretty town to walk around, the people friendly too as they passed her with a smile or a word of greeting. Most of all it was normal, something that Skye also didn't seem to have had for a very long time.

She was a little taken aback, though, as she returned to the square a short time later with her purchases to see Falkner standing beside the Range Rover in conversation with a rather vivacious brunette.

Although why she should be jealous Skye had no idea; she should know better than anyone, loving him as she did, how attractive Falkner was to women!

But the other woman's presence did put her in something of a quandary. Should she rejoin Falkner anyway, or leave him to have his conversation in private?

Part of her said she was being silly, that the sensible thing was just to rejoin him as if she found nothing unusual in his talking to the other woman. But another part of her said she didn't want confirmation that the rather beautiful brunette was actually the current woman in Falkner's life.

Just because there was no woman in residence at Falkner's home, did not mean he wasn't involved with someone. In fact, after his casual remark about his injuries not being a problem to him when he was 'lying horizontal', the likelihood was very much the opposite!

Coward, she told herself impatiently. Just because Falkner was smiling broadly at the other woman, his eyes crinkling at the corners, his whole demeanour one of warmth, did not mean he was involved with the woman.

Or did it? She really was a baby when it came to reading the signs of a relationship, her only experience of it so far the marriage between her uncle Seamus and Shanna—and that had been volatile from the first.

Just walk casually over there and join them, Skye told herself firmly, knowing she couldn't stand here skulking on the street corner for ever; several people had already eyed her curiously as it was.

The brunette had her back turned towards Skye as she crossed the street to the square, but Falkner saw her approach over the other woman's shoulder, his face brightening with recognition.

Quickly followed by—was that a guarded look Skye could now see in his eyes? Well, it was too bad if it was; by crossing the street at all she was committed to joining them now.

'Ah, there you are,' Falkner greeted—rather more jovially than was necessary, Skye thought with a frown.

The brunette instantly turned too, the warm smile fading from her lips as her eyes widened in obvious shock. 'Selina…!' she gasped incredulously.

Skye frowned her consternation. 'No, I—'

'Belinda, this is Skye O'Hara,' Falkner was the one to cut in firmly, moving slightly so that he now stood at Skye's side. 'Skye, this is Belinda—'

'Oh, I'm so sorry,' the other woman burst out awkwardly. 'It was just—for a moment, with the sun behind you like that, and the red hair— But of course you aren't Selina,' she dismissed with a forced smile. 'Did you say Skye O'Hara, Falkner?' she realized suddenly, turning to him frowningly.

Close to like this, Skye could see that the other woman was older than she had first thought, probably somewhere in her early to mid-thirties. Not that that would matter to Falkner; in fact she was much more his own age than Skye was.

It was more than a little odd that the woman had initially thought she was Selina, though. That had been the name of Falkner's wife, hadn't it…? And as far as she was aware, Selina had departed from Falkner's life years ago. Although she had apparently been a redhead, too…

But she forgot all about that as Falkner answered the other woman firmly. 'Yes, I did say that.' His gaze was fixed warningly on Belinda, it now seemed to Skye.

Belinda recovered herself quickly, smiling brightly. 'What a pretty name.'

Skye had bristled defensively as she'd seen the look that passed between Falkner and the woman Belinda, not fooled for a moment by her friendliness; Belinda had obviously heard her name before even if she hadn't actually recognized her, and not under flattering circumstances if that perplexed frown had been anything to go by.

'Skye or O'Hara?' she came back challengingly.

A delicate blush heightened Belinda's cheeks now, Skye instantly regretting her challenge as she saw the embarrassed confusion clearly written on the other woman's face. Goodness knew, she should be hardened to people recognizing her name, if not her face, by now!

'We have to be going now, I'm afraid, Belinda,' Falkner was the one to answer, at the same time his hand moving out to grasp the top of Skye's arm and pin her firmly to his side.

Belinda blinked, shaking her head slightly before she turned to look at Falkner. 'I told the kids I would bring them over to see you after school if you were back?' She looked at him questioningly.

'I'm back,' Falkner drawled.

Belinda still frowned. 'So I can bring them over?'

'Why not?' Falkner shrugged.

'It was nice meeting you, Skye.' The other woman turned to smile at her.

'You'll be meeting her again in a few minutes, Belinda,' Falkner told the other woman lightly. 'Skye is staying at the house with me,' he explained at her questioning look.

Skye was still reeling over the mention of 'the kids'. What kids? Surely they couldn't be Falkner's children? As far as Skye was aware, he had only been married the once, and there certainly weren't any children from that brief marriage!

But she was snapped out of these musings as Falkner's hand tightened pointedly on her arm, turning to smile blandly at the other woman. 'It appears I'll see you later, too, then,' she returned politely.

Even if she didn't have any idea who the other woman was. Or what she meant to Falkner!

CHAPTER FIVE

'SHE'S my sister, Skye.'

Skye had been so deep in thought as they drove the short distance to his home, at the other woman's puzzling mistake concerning her identity, at the fact that Belinda had at least obviously heard of Skye's real name, at exactly what role the beautiful Belinda played in Falkner's life, that it took a few minutes for Falkner's words to penetrate her misery.

His sister?

Had he really just said that the vivaciously beautiful Belinda was his sister?

'Obviously my younger sister,' Falkner continued dryly. 'The kids she's bringing over shortly are my niece and nephew, Melissa and Jeremy. Or Lissa and Jemmy, as the family affectionately call them.'

Had it been that obvious to him that the puzzle of exactly where Belinda and 'the kids' fitted into his life bothered her? It really wouldn't do if it had... Falkner was being extremely kind to her by taking her to stay at his home, he certainly didn't need the complication of realizing she had foolishly been in love with him all these years!

Skye swallowed hard, forcing herself to give a bright smile. 'She seems very nice,' she returned noncommittally, at the same time desperately re-evaluating Falkner's relationship to the other woman.

Falkner gave her a mocking glance. 'She is.' He nodded. 'She's also extremely curious now about where you fit into my life,' he added dryly.

Skye's eyes widened. 'How can you possibly know that?' Belinda hadn't even known Skye was with Falkner until that last few minutes.

'She's my sister, Skye.' He shrugged. 'All sisters are romantically curious about any woman they see with their brothers,' he added from experience.

'I see.' Skye chewed on her bottom lip. 'I didn't mean to make things—awkward, for you, with your family.'

He chuckled softly. 'You haven't.' He gave a rueful shake of his head. 'Belinda has been matchmaking for me for as long as I can remember—to no avail,' he added hardly.

Skye couldn't help wondering if Belinda had been involved in Falkner's initial meeting with Selina…? If she had, it was no wonder he now viewed her matchmaking with a jaundiced eye.

'I'm sure she means well,' Skye dismissed.

'So did Lucretia Borgia, probably,' he came back derisively.

Skye burst out laughing at the comparison, sobering to shake her head. 'I don't think Lucretia actually did any matchmaking for other people—she was too busy being married off by her politically ambitious father and brother.' In fact Skye had always had a sneaking sympathy for the maligned Lucretia, considered her to have been a pawn in the Borgia family rather than being directly involved in their machinations.

Falkner eyed her admiringly. 'I stand corrected,' he drawled. 'But, either way, Belinda's efforts are wasted where I'm concerned,' he added determinedly.

Now it was Skye's turn to eye him curiously. 'Once bitten, twice shy, is that it?'

Falkner stiffened, his expression becoming aloofly remote. 'I believe that question comes under the heading of "personal", Skye,' he rasped harshly.

She paled at the rebuke. Although she accepted it was probably deserved. Except... Falkner already knew so much about her own personal life, she couldn't help feeling curious about his.

Although, if she thought about it, she already knew that both his parents were alive and living in Florida, that he had a sister called Belinda who obviously lived close by with her family.

But they weren't what she would call insightful things, not like the personal details he knew of her own life. Besides, feeling about him as she did, she couldn't help but feel curious about his brief marriage...

'I'm sorry.' She shrugged.

Falkner gave a heavy sigh. 'Skye, until I was forced to retire from professional showjumping three years ago, my life was an open book, with nothing, it seemed, too personal to appear in print. When Selina and I were separated shortly afterwards it made the headlines too, but then it all quietened down. The divorce started it all up again a year later. You can't know the blessed relief of these last two years of relative anonymity!'

Couldn't she? What he had described had happened to her in reverse; most of her life spent peacefully with her father, the last six months becoming a publicity nightmare. Yes, she perfectly understood Falkner's desire for anonymity.

She grimaced. 'If that's the way you feel, then you really shouldn't have come to the hospital to see me, of all people, let alone brought me home with you!' In fact, she was surprised there weren't reporters camped outside his home, waiting for a glimpse of Connor O'Hara's daughter, right now!

Falkner eyed her ruefully. 'And what sort of friend would that make me?' he derided.

'A sensible one?' she suggested dryly.

He grinned. 'You know, Skye, if I were of a more sensitive nature, I could be quite hurt by your obvious reluctance to be anywhere near me!'

How wrong he was about that! Falkner was exactly the person she wanted to be with. The same person she had wanted to be with for the last six years!

She shook her head. 'I wasn't talking about me, Falkner,' she chided impatiently. 'They seem to be a little tardy at the moment, but once the press realize I'm staying at your home—!' She grimaced. 'Your anonymity will be blown for a while, I'm afraid.'

'Oh, don't be afraid, Skye,' Falkner assured her hardly. 'I'm all grown up, I can take all the flak they choose to throw my way. As for being tardy…' He paused. 'I doubt you realized it, Skye, but we left the estate this morning by a rather obscure way. The same way we're going back in,' he told her softly as he turned the Range Rover onto the rutted track. 'The reason for that being that I've been reliably informed that certain members of the press are lying in wait for us at the front entrance.'

Skye sank back in her seat like a deflated balloon.

She had noticed they hadn't left earlier by the front entrance, of course, but had just assumed this was an easier way to get into town. It certainly hadn't occurred to her that there could be a much more sinister reason for them doing so.

'How did you stand it, Falkner?' she choked, burying her face in her hands. 'How much more of it can I stand?' she groaned emotionally, the loss of her father once again pressing down on her.

The first that she knew about Falkner stopping the vehicle was when he took her into his arms. 'As much as it takes, Skye,' he murmured gently into the silky softness of her hair. 'You're doing very well, you know,' he added huskily as she made no response except to burrow comfortingly into those reassuring arms.

She raised her tear-wet face at this. 'I'm doing very well?' she repeated brokenly. 'Oh, Falkner!' She shook her head. 'How can you possibly say that when all I really want to do is find a quiet place and hide myself there until this is all over?'

He grasped her arms lightly. 'Because you're still here and not there,' he told her firmly. 'Skye, do you think I don't know how you feel? Of course I do! But the truth of the matter is that you won't run away and hide, that you will stay right here—because you know that's what Connor would have wanted you to do!'

He was right, of course. Despite the problems at O'Hara Whiskey, the rumours that had followed, the speculation in the newspapers, the shareholders' outrage, all the bad publicity that had gone along with that, her father had continued to live his life as openly as he had always done, had refused to be cowed by any of it. Exactly as she was now doing in his stead.

Falkner looked at her intently, the steeliness of that blue gaze willing her to go on, not to give in to those feelings of panic that made her just want to cut and run.

And, in truth, she couldn't really just cut and run. If for no other reason than that she had her father's funeral to attend in three days' time…

She straightened, Falkner's hands dropping away from her arms as she did so. Although she could still feel the warmth of his touch against her sensitized flesh… 'I'm sorry.' She sighed. 'About the outburst. I—I'll try not to do it again.' She swallowed hard, her chin raised determinedly now.

Falkner straightened in his own car seat before nodding abruptly. 'I know you will,' he murmured huskily. 'But I—I'm here, if you need me, Skye. Try to remember that, will you?' Once again his gaze was intense on the paleness of her face.

She gave the ghost of a smile. 'I'll remember.'

'Good enough,' Falkner acknowledged briskly before once again starting the engine and continuing the drive to the back of the house.

'Falkner…?' Skye voiced slowly a few seconds later, her emotions once again under control.

'Hmm?' he prompted distractedly.

'Yesterday you said—you said you had seen me during the last six months?' She looked at him expectantly.

He glanced at her frowningly before his mouth twisted into the semblance of a smile. 'Why is it that women seem to have perfect recall for every remark a man ever made to them?' He gave a derisive shake of his head.

'Whereas men never remember a single thing a woman says to them?' she came back tauntingly.

His smile deepened. 'We remember the important things.'

'Such as?' she teased.

'Such as—such as—'

'Hah!' she pounced pointedly. 'And you still haven't answered my question,' she reminded lightly.

'I've forgotten what it was now!' Falkner returned teasingly. 'You—look at that; we've been so long getting back that Belinda and the children are already here,' he pointed out wryly.

Skye turned to see a green station wagon was parked on the driveway in front of the house, realizing this must belong to Falkner's sister.

'How convenient,' Skye murmured dryly.

Falkner parked the Range Rover beside the station wagon before turning to give a mocking inclination of his head. 'Sisters do have their uses after all,' he drawled mockingly.

Skye determined as she climbed out of the Range Rover that she would return to the subject of Falkner having seen her at some time during the last six months at a more convenient time. If Falkner thought he had got away with not answering her at all then he was in for a surprise!

But there was no time to tell him that as the equivalent of two small tornadoes came hurtling out of the house, both determined to be the first to launch themselves into Falkner's arms.

'Steady!' he murmured as the two small children almost knocked him off his feet. 'I've only been away for three days, not three years!' he teased as he held up a child in each arm.

Something that Skye was sure couldn't be all that good for his damaged leg...

Lissa and Jemmy, both dark-haired and blue-eyed, were obviously twins, probably aged about six. They were also robust and solidly made for six-year-olds!

'Get down, you two.' Their long-suffering mother had followed them out of the house, pausing at the top of the steps to raise dark brows until Lissa and Jemmy were returned to the gravel driveway to stand on their own sturdy feet. 'Better,' Belinda told them briskly. 'Now say hello politely to Uncle Fork's guest,' she added pointedly.

The two children looked up sheepishly at Skye, Lissa obviously the leader of the two as she suddenly grinned boldly, Jemmy having moved so that he stood slightly behind his uncle Fork's long legs looking out at her.

'Hello, you two.' Skye smiled as she took the initiative. 'Lissa and Jemmy, isn't it? And I'm Skye.'

Jemmy raised his gaze uncertainly skywards, and then back at Skye, obviously a little unsure of this introduction.

'Because you have blue eyes like the sky!' Lissa felt no such inhibitions.

Skye gave Falkner a pointed look, as much as to say, You see, even a child knows how I came by my name!

'Yes, I do,' Skye confirmed smilingly.

'We've come to tea,' Lissa informed her brightly. 'Haven't we, Uncle Fork?' She looked up at him trustingly as she neatly tucked her hand inside his much larger one.

'So it would appear,' he accepted ruefully. 'In fact, I wouldn't be surprised if Mrs Graham isn't getting it ready right now.'

'Are you sure you want to be bothered with them today?' Belinda frowned her concern.

Because she was here, Skye realised. But she had

already decided that she liked Falkner's sister, and the twins were absolutely enchanting as they stood either side of Falkner now, each with a hand resting trustingly in his.

'Do you think there will be jam sandwiches for tea?' Skye prompted the twins excitedly. 'I love jam sandwiches!'

'So do I,' Jemmy was the one to answer her shyly. 'Strawberry ones.'

'Oh, definitely strawberry,' Skye agreed as she preceded them up the stone steps to where Belinda stood watching them.

'And chocolate cake,' Lissa put in happily, not to be outdone by her twin.

'My favourite.' Skye nodded, turning to smile at Belinda. 'Your children are adorable!' she told the other woman softly.

Belinda grimaced. 'You should try looking after them for a week!' But the look of maternal affection she bestowed on her offspring totally belied her words.

'I already have,' Falkner drawled. 'I still have the scars to prove it!' he added dryly.

'I think Uncle Fork is teasing you,' Skye told the twins laughingly. 'Aren't you, Uncle Fork?' She raised mocking brows.

Somehow, hearing Falkner addressed in this totally affectionate way by his family, in the company of two such adorable children as Lissa and Jemmy, Skye thought the world didn't seem such a dark, dismal place after all...

'I think,' Falkner murmured softly in her ear as they all entered the house, 'that you and Uncle Fork had better have a quiet chat together later.'

'Really?' Skye returned as softly, aware that the others

couldn't hear their conversation, although the more astute Belinda was looking at the two of them curiously.

'Really,' Falkner echoed pointedly.

She gave him a teasing smile. 'I'll look forward to it!'

'Uncle Fork, did you bring us a present back from Ireland?' Lissa prompted expectantly.

'Melissa Chapman!' Her mother looked down at her reprovingly. 'What have I told you about asking for presents?'

'"Wait until people offer them, and then say thank you nicely",' Lissa obviously quoted perfectly. 'I was only asking in case Uncle Fork forgot,' she explained reasonably.

Falkner's mouth twitched as he obviously had trouble holding back a smile. 'You're quite right, Lissa, I had forgotten.' He nodded. 'I believe there's a present for each of you on the desk in my study—' Before he could even finish speaking the two children had set off at a run down the hallway that obviously led to his study.

Falkner burst out laughing, and a few seconds later his sister reluctantly joined in.

'They really are incorrigible.' Belinda shook her head ruefully. 'I'm so sorry about this, Skye.'

Skye hadn't particularly been aware of the conversation taking place the last few minutes, had become caught up in her own thoughts at Lissa's mention of Falkner's trip to Ireland. Obviously his family were aware of where he had been for three days, but did they also know that it had been on her behalf? The twins, probably not. But what of Belinda?

She forced herself to abandon those thoughts long enough to reassure the older woman. 'You have nothing to apologize for. I told you, I think your children are wonderful.' Besides, she was the interloper here; it was obvious from their familiarity that the twins came here to tea on a regular basis when Falkner was at home.

It was the twins' exuberance that made the next hour pass in easy relaxation, Lissa chattering away about her new doll, Jemmy fascinated by his new transforming toy, the two of them rapidly devouring the tea Mrs Graham had set out for them in the kitchen.

In fact, Skye felt so comfortable in their presence that she wasn't in the least put out when Falkner had to go to his study to take a telephone call.

'I'm terribly sorry about—about your recent loss, Skye,' Belinda told her softly, her words such that she didn't incur the children's curiosity as they tucked into their chocolate cake.

Skye swallowed hard. 'Thank you.' Her voice was husky as she inwardly acknowledged that the other woman knew exactly who she was. Who her father was. 'I don't know what I would have done without Falkner's help this last few days.' Her gaze remained unwaveringly on the older woman.

Belinda nodded. 'He and your father were good friends.'

So it would appear. Which made it all the stranger that Skye hadn't been aware of their continued friendship once Falkner had retired from showjumping three years ago...

'Yes,' she returned noncommittally.

'Not that I'm saying the two of you aren't,' Belinda rushed into embarrassed speech. 'It's just that I knew about your father because I met him here several times myself—'

'Belinda, do you think I could have a quiet word

with you before you have to leave?' A poker-faced Falkner stood in the kitchen doorway.

His face might be expressionless, but nevertheless Skye could feel the waves of displeasure emanating from him. As could Belinda, if the haste with which she left the kitchen to join her brother was anything to go by.

Not exactly subtle on Falkner's part, Skye acknowledged with a grimace; his conversation with his sister would obviously be about her.

Or was she just being oversensitive? After all, this was the first time brother and sister had seen each other for almost a week; they probably had things they wished to discuss away from curious little ears. Besides, wasn't she being a little conceited to assume Falkner might have anything to say to his sister about her?

Maybe so, but when Belinda hadn't returned ten minutes later Skye excused herself to the twins of the pretext of needing the bathroom, sure that the children would be perfectly happy left in the indulgent Mrs Graham's company for a few minutes.

She wasn't really meaning to eavesdrop, had actually gone in search of Falkner and Belinda without alarming the children because she wondered, in view of their long absence, if there was anything wrong. But as Skye approached Falkner's study, the door standing slightly ajar, she heard Belinda speaking inside the room, those words making Skye freeze outside in the hallway.

'—must know that Skye will have to be told what's happening, Falkner,' Belinda said reprovingly.

'And you think now is the right time for that, do you?' he came back hardly.

'Is there ever going to be a good time?' his sister returned ruefully.

'The funeral is in three days time, Belinda; let's leave it until after then, hmm?' Falkner rasped determinedly.

'I can't see how leaving it is going to change things—'

'I don't remember asking for your advice, Belinda,' Falkner bit out harshly. 'Only your cooperation!'

Skye knew that if Falkner spoke to her in that coldly determined way she would just want to shrivel up and die; and from Belinda's silence after this outburst, she was more than a little shocked by her brother's steeliness too!

'I'm sorry, Lindy.' Falkner sighed heavily. 'I shouldn't take any of this out on you. But if you had any idea of the strain I'm under at the moment...!'

'Having met Skye, I can take a pretty accurate guess,' his sister came back dryly.

'Belinda, don't add two and two together and come up with five, hmm?' he derided.

'Oh, I think just making the four will do it,' Belinda assured him wryly. 'Falkner, why—what was that?' she said sharply. 'I thought I heard a noise outside?' she added worriedly.

In fact, the noise Belinda had heard was the twins as they came hurtling down the hallway in search of their mother and uncle, obviously having demolished the tea to their satisfaction and now ready for home.

Caught in the middle, as Skye obviously was, she knew she couldn't just continue to stand out here in the hallway, guessed that, if Lissa and Jemmy didn't reach her first, at any moment either Belinda or Falkner were going to come out of the study in search of the noise Belinda had heard and realize that she had been standing out here listening to their conversation.

'Careful.' She turned smilingly to the twins as they

looked in danger of crashing into her in their exuberance. Only just in time, Skye realized with an inward groan as Falkner wrenched the study door open, a frown marring his brow as he saw the three of them standing there. 'The twins were wondering where the two of you had got to,' she told Falkner lightly.

He continued to frown, eyes narrowed on her questioningly, obviously not absolutely convinced by this explanation.

'I was just telling Falkner that we would have to leave now,' Belinda spoke up brightly as she came to the doorway to join her brother. 'Otherwise Daddy will be wondering why he doesn't have any dinner waiting for him when he gets home,' she told the twins teasingly.

Skye frowned at the other woman, knowing that Belinda hadn't just been telling Falkner anything of the kind. What had that conversation between brother and sister meant? What was Falkner keeping from her? And why?

'Actually, Skye,' Belinda continued lightly, 'I was just reminding Falkner about the barbecue we're having on Sunday for the twins' sixth birthday. Which, of course, you're invited to. Falkner didn't seem to think it was a good idea to mention it at the moment...'

Skye looked frowningly at the other woman. This explanation certainly fitted in with the little of the conversation she had overheard between brother and sister.

And yet...

CHAPTER SIX

'ONLY a couple of hours, Skye, and then all this will be over,' Falkner reassured her gently as he sat beside her.

'All this' being her father's very private funeral!

Skye had been waiting in the sitting-room with Falkner when the car had arrived outside the house promptly at two-thirty, the two of them even now sitting in the family car as they drove to the church, Belinda and her husband Charles, as the only other mourners, following behind in the second car.

'I'll be with you the whole time,' Falkner assured her as he reached out and took her hand in the warmth of his. 'You're freezing!' he realized concernedly.

Frozen probably best described the way Skye felt right now. Numbed. Emotionally as well as physically. It was the only way she could possibly deal with the next couple of hours.

Her tension had been steadily increasing over the last three days, so much so that in the end Falkner had given up even trying to make conversation with her. But at the same time he had never left her alone, always making sure either Mrs Graham or Belinda were with her if he had to go out anywhere.

Quite what he thought she was going to do if left to her own devices, Skye had no idea, but she was nevertheless grateful for the sympathetic company, silent though it often was.

Although today was turning out just as horrific as she had thought it would be, reporters surrounding the car as they came out of the driveway, several of them seeming to have jumped into cars so that they could follow them.

'Skye—'

'I'm fine, Falkner,' she told him harshly, teeth gritted to stop their chattering. 'Just fine,' she repeated, her gaze fixed determinedly ahead.

It was the only part of her that was looking ahead; inwardly Skye couldn't see past the service. Although Falkner had said that her father's lawyer would be coming to the house on their return, for the reading of the will. Something else she had little interest in; by the time her father died, his love had been the only thing of value he could leave her.

'Uncle Seamus should have been here.' She spoke her thoughts out loud, her voice sounding strangely hollow in the silence.

Falkner's mouth tightened. 'He should have been, yes.'

Skye turned to him with pained eyes. 'He's my father's only other living relative.'

Falkner snorted. 'A good example of "you can choose your friends but you can't choose your relatives"!'

Her uncle Seamus really hadn't made a good impression on Falkner when he'd visited Ireland the weekend before. Which was a pity, because Uncle Seamus was her only living relative now.

She fell silent again, remaining so during the rest of

the drive, her hand tightly gripped in Falkner's as he
fought his way through the reporters waiting at the
church, that hand remaining in his through the nightmare of the service.

And beyond.

'When will it stop, Falkner?' She finally broke down
once they had returned to the house two hours later, her
father laid to rest beside her mother, a woman Skye had
never known, but the woman her father had continued
to love until his own death. 'When will they leave me
alone?' The reporters had dogged them as they'd come
out of the church and back to the house.

'We'll wait for you in the conservatory,' Belinda
murmured softly to Falkner, her arm linked with her
husband, Charles's, as they left Skye and Falkner alone
in the sitting-room.

Falkner took Skye gently into his arms, cradling her
head against his shoulder. 'No one is going to hurt you
while I'm around, Skye,' he assured her huskily.

But he wouldn't always be around, at some stage she
had to take up the reins of a life for herself. Would those
story-hungry reporters still be lying in wait for her even
then? Her father's life had been in ruins before he'd
died; wasn't that enough?

Falkner drew in a deep breath at her silence. 'Skye,
there are some things I have to tell you, to ask you—'

'Falkner, I'm really sorry to interrupt you,' Belinda cut
in with obvious reluctance. 'But the lawyer has arrived.'

Skye looked up sharply. 'I can't do this now, Falkner,'
she pleaded, her eyes swimming with tears. 'I just can't!'

'Of course she can't,' Belinda protested con cernedly
as she came further into the room to take Skye into her
own arms. 'He'll have to come back another time,' she

told her brother firmly. 'What Skye needs right now is peace and quiet, to be surrounded by the people who care about her.'

The problem with that was that Skye didn't seem to have any people to care about her: her father was dead, her uncle Seamus still in hospital. Oh, she knew that Falkner, and his family, had been kind to her, and she appreciated it, but that would all come to an end soon.

She had never felt so alone, so utterly bereft—

'You deal with it, will you, Belinda?' Falkner told his sister distractedly, his worried gaze fixed on Skye as she walked zombie-like across the room to stare unseeingly out of the window.

'Of course,' Belinda assured briskly. 'But, Falkner—'

'I know, Lindy,' he sighed heavily.

Skye was barely aware of Falkner and Belinda, that feeling of floating, of not quite being there, intensifying as she looked in on the bleakness of her life.

She would stay until after the funeral, she had told Falkner when she'd first come home with him. Well, that was now. So what did she do? Where did she go? Ireland seemed the most sensible—only?—place to go. But, as Falkner had already pointed out, what was really there for her? Her uncle Seamus might need her for a short time when he came out of hospital, but even that would only be delaying the inevitable; she had to find a job, some way of supporting herself.

Worst of all, when she left here she wouldn't see Falkner again!

'Skye...?' He came up behind her now, his hands moving up to lightly clasp the tops of her arms.

She swallowed hard, fighting the desire she had to turn and throw herself into his arms; that would just embarrass both of them! 'I don't care what any of them say, my father was a good man,' she told him defiantly.

'Yes, he was,' Falkner confirmed huskily.

She glanced at him frowningly. 'Why is it that you believe that and no one else does?' She looked up at him imploringly.

He shrugged. 'Probably because they didn't know your father like we did,' he murmured softly.

'Oh, Falkner!' she groaned emotionally, almost collapsing against him as she felt him take her gently into his arms, her head resting against his shoulder as he lightly caressed the hair at her nape.

'It will get better, Skye,' he told her reassuringly. 'Right now everything looks very—dark—' he sighed '—but it will get better,' he repeated firmly.

She looked up at him with tear-wet eyes. 'Will it?'

'It has to.' Falkner nodded, kissing her lightly on her brow. 'When you reach the bottom the only way to go is up!' he added ruefully.

'You think?' she choked.

'I know it,' he assured her with feeling. 'Skye, you're young, and beautiful, and you deserve the best that life can give you.'

He was the best thing that life could ever give her, but she very much doubted he would ever be hers.

She moved slightly away from him, needing to put a little space between them—before she completely disgraced herself! 'Those reporters out there—they're like hounds baying when they scent their prey. What's wrong with them?' she added disgustedly.

Falkner drew in a sharp breath. 'Skye, there are some things you don't know—'

She gave a shaky laugh. 'Falkner, the length and

breadth of what I don't know would reach from here to—'

'Not those sort of things,' he humoured her lightly. 'Skye, let's sit down, hmm?' he encouraged as he moved away from her. 'I need to talk to you. And I think I can do that better if you sit there and I sit over here,' he added self-derisively.

Skye eyed him frowningly as she moved to sit in the chair he indicated across the fireplace from the one he chose to sit in, crossing one silky knee over the other, her hands laced primly together in the lap of her skirt. She felt like a schoolgirl waiting for a reprimand from the headmaster!

Except, she had no idea what she had done...

'Yes?' she prompted when Falkner seemed to be having a little difficulty putting his thoughts into words.

An unusual circumstance in itself; she had never known Falkner at a loss for words before!

Looking at him, she could see that the last few days hadn't been easy ones for him, either. There were dark shadows under his eyes, lines grooved into his cheeks beside his grimly set mouth, a wariness about him that she was pretty sure wasn't his usual demeanour.

'You may as well tell me, Falkner,' she encouraged heavily. 'If not, I'm only going to imagine the worst!' If there could be anything worse than these last two weeks!

'Okay!' He gave a humourless smile. 'Skye, I—I want you to give some thought to the idea of marrying me.'

She didn't move, didn't so much as blink, merely continued to look at him. Whatever she had been expecting him to say, it certainly wasn't this!

Had Falkner really just asked her to marry him? Heaven knew she had thought of being his wife any amount of times these last six years, of having him in love with her, of telling him how much she loved him. But that wasn't quite what Falkner had said, was it…?

He had asked her to 'give some thought to the idea of marrying him', which was something else entirely.

'For goodness' sake say something, Skye!' he finally muttered derisively.

She drew in a shaky breath. 'Why?'

He blinked. 'Why say something? Or why—?'

'Why should I give some thought to the idea of marrying you?' she corrected impatiently, sure that he already knew exactly what she had meant. But he was delaying answering her. Why?

He stood up impatiently, thrusting his hands into his trouser pockets. 'Why not?' he rasped harshly. 'Oh, I'll admit, I'm probably not quite your idea of the ideal husband. I'm too old for you, for one thing, and the accident three years ago pretty well shattered one of my legs, but I am rich, rich enough to take care of you, and—'

'Stop right there!' Skye ordered forcefully as she too stood up, more and more convinced that there was something dreadfully wrong about Falkner's marriage proposal; it had no declaration of love to accompany it, for one thing…! 'Falkner, what is going on? Why are you asking me to marry you?' She stared at him with compelling eyes.

He raised dark brows. 'You don't think it's because you're a beautiful young woman—'

'No, I don't,' she cut in forcefully. 'Nor do I think that it's because you've fallen madly in love with me,' she dismissed scathingly.

He grimaced. 'I knew I should have got down on the

customary one knee—but I thought it might be embarrassing, for both of us, when I wasn't able to get up again!'

Skye didn't return his self-derisive smile, sure that he was just delaying answering her.

She would be lying if she didn't acknowledge that when Falkner had first mentioned the word marriage, her heart had leapt hopefully, but there had been nothing in his demeanour then, or now, that gave any indication he had proposed to her because he was in love with her. So why was he asking her to marry him…?

She gave an impatient shake of her head. 'Something else is going on here, Falkner—and I think it's time you told me what it is!'

She had sensed all along that there was something odd about the way Falkner had turned up at the hospital in the way he had, whisking her off to his home the last five days, even more strangely, brought Storm over from Ireland. But his marriage proposal, coming completely out of the blue like this, had to be the strangest thing he had done so far.

Skye looked at Falkner expectantly as he drew in a ragged breath, hardly able to contain her impatience when his gaze moved past her to his sister as she appeared hesitantly in the doorway.

'I'm really sorry to interrupt the two of you again.' Belinda grimaced sheepishly. 'I've dealt with the lawyer.' She spoke directly to her brother. 'Now I'm afraid Charles and I will have to be going.' She gave Skye an apologetic smile. 'Charles's mother has been looking after the kids since she collected them from school, but she isn't too well at the moment, so I don't like to leave them with her for too long.'

'I appreciate you and Charles being here at all,

Belinda,' Skye assured the older woman, crossing the room to give Belinda a brief hug. 'You've both been wonderful this last few days,' she added huskily; she had met Charles for the first time yesterday evening, when he and Belinda had joined them for dinner.

'I was glad to be of help,' Belinda told her warmly. 'Don't bother to see us out; we'll give you a call later this evening, Falkner.' She moved to kiss her brother lightly on the cheek.

The silence in the room was electric once Belinda had gone, the tension between Skye and Falkner so high the very air seemed to crackle with it.

'Falkner?' Skye finally snapped when she could take the silence no longer. 'Would you like to tell me now why it is that you're offering me some sort of marriage of convenience?' Her eyes sparkled with her inner outrage at such a proposal. But what else, in the circumstances, was she to think?

His mouth twisted ruefully. 'Believe me, Skye, I don't consider any marriage a "convenience"!'

No, after the disaster his first marriage had obviously been, he probably didn't. In fact, Skye was sure that the idea of marrying again was not something Falkner had even considered. Until now.

'You're prevaricating,' she told him tightly.

'Of course I'm prevaricating!' he burst out impatiently, his whole body tense with anger. 'Your reaction to my suggestion hasn't exactly been positive, now, has it? In fact, from the way you're behaving, anyone would think I was offering to set you up as my mistress somewhere!'

Her eyes flashed deeply blue. 'Instead of which you're offering me the coldness of—'

'A marriage of convenience,' he finished furiously,

crossing the room in two strides to pull her into his arms, his mouth coming down forcefully on hers.

It was as if the last six years had never happened, was just as it had been that first time Falkner had kissed her; every bone in her body seemed to melt, every inch of her flesh feeling as if it were on fire, the blood pounding heatedly through her veins.

Her arms moved compulsively about his shoulders, her hands threading into the thickness of his hair as she kissed him back with all the pent-up longing inside her.

He felt so good, so exactly right, his body curved into hers, her nipples pressed against the hardness of his chest, their heartbeats sounding as one as it pounded in her ears.

Skye's mouth parted hungrily beneath his, the tip of his tongue moving questioningly along her bottom lip, and, finding no opposition, entering the moist warmth beneath.

Her pulse leapt as she urged even closer against him, her nipples hard now, the heat of her thighs moving against the hardness of his, Falkner's hands cradling either side of her face now as his mouth thoroughly explored hers.

Skye gasped as one of those hands moved to cup beneath a pouting breast, his thumbtip moving against a hardened nipple, fiery pleasure such as she had never known before surging through her.

She wanted him, how she wanted him, completely, in every way possible!

Her hands tightened on his shoulders as his mouth left hers to move hotly to the creamy column of her throat, teeth lightly biting the soft lobe of her ear, his breath hot like burning lava against her sensitized skin. At the same time, his hand moving urgently against the tenderness of her breast, his roused thighs telling her of his own need.

'"Cold", Skye?' he suddenly groaned. 'Somehow I don't think so!' he added urgently.

His words had the same effect as an ice cube down her back, Skye wrenching away to look up at him, her eyes black smudges in the otherwise paleness of her face.

Falkner held onto her upper arms as he looked back at her, a nerve pulsing in the hardness of his cheek as he refused to release her. 'Would marrying me really be so bad, Skye?' he prompted harshly. 'Would it?' He shook her slightly. 'You could have a good life here as my wife. No financial worries, the freedom to be what you want, go where you want, see who you want. And there's plenty of room here for you to ride Storm.'

It wouldn't be bad at all—in fact, Skye could imagine nothing she wanted more. But not like this. Never like this.

She wrenched away from him, breathing hard in her agitation. 'You still haven't told me why, Falkner,' she reminded forcefully.

He flung up his arms, moving agitatedly away from her. 'For the reasons I've just stated! Because I want to look after you, protect you—'

'From what?' she cried. 'What is so scary out there—' she moved a hand restlessly to the outside world '—that you feel you have to marry me to protect me from it?'

Falkner became suddenly still, that nerve once again pulsing in his tightly clenched jaw. 'Nothing. There's nothing out there, Skye,' he continued hardly as she would have interrupted. 'No business. No home. Certainly no concerned uncle,' he added with scathing displeasure.

Skye became suddenly still, frowning her puzzlement as she looked searchingly at Falkner. What did he mean? The business was finished, yes, which meant she would have to find a job to support herself. But her home, the home that had been in the O'Hara family for generations, was still there—wasn't it? As to her uncle Seamus, he would be out of hospital this weekend—wouldn't he?

Falkner ran a hand restlessly through the thickness of his hair. 'It's all gone, Skye,' he rasped. 'Everything your great-grandfather, grandfather and father worked for, all those years. All of it wiped out by the greed of one man,' he added disgustedly.

Her eyes flashed as she shook her head in sharp denial. 'I told you, my father didn't do the things they said—'

'Not your father, Skye,' Falkner cut in impatiently. 'I'm sure I've already assured you that I totally believed in Connor's innocence of the mismanagement he was accused of. The thing is—' he sighed heavily '—there's plenty of evidence now to confirm it's no longer just a belief.'

'What—?'

'Skye, there was a very good reason why your uncle Seamus wasn't able to be at the funeral today,' Falkner continued with grim determination.

She frowned her confusion. 'You told me he's in hospital with a broken leg…?'

'If I could get my hands on him he would have a broken neck to go with it!' Falkner bit out harshly. 'Unfortunately, his case is now in the hands of the police. Which means Seamus O'Hara is well out of my reach!'

'The police…?' she repeated uncomprehendingly.

Falkner nodded abruptly. 'Skye, your uncle Seamus was formally charged earlier in the week after admitting to the police that he was the one who embezzled the money from O'Hara Whiskey, of defrauding the company and its shareholders. He was the one responsible for the company downfall, and in the process, for ruining your father and his reputation!' Falkner was breathing hard in his agitation.

Skye could only stare open-mouthed at Falkner, unable to take in the enormity of what he was telling her.

It couldn't be true, could it...?

CHAPTER SEVEN

'I DON'T believe you,' Skye denied stiltedly, her hands up over her ears as she backed disbelievingly away from Falkner.

Those things he had said about her uncle couldn't be true. They couldn't!

Falkner took a step towards her, coming to an abrupt halt as she just moved further away from him. 'Skye, there is no easy way for me to tell you any of these things.' He groaned regrettably. 'I've managed to keep the truth from you the last week or so, by making sure that no newspapers got into your hospital room, no telephone calls for the same reason—'

'You did that?' Skye gasped incredulously, having had no idea, not a single suspicion that this had been going on in the background.

'Yes, I did,' he confirmed challengingly. 'I also did the same thing once you were here. And I would do it all again if I had to,' he told her assuredly. 'But sooner or later someone is going to slip up, say something they shouldn't, leave a newspaper lying around that you shouldn't see, turn on the television—'

'Mrs Graham and Belinda have been in on this too,' she

realized dazedly, saw now exactly what Belinda's conversation in Falkner's study a few days ago had been about!

'But only at my request.' Falkner nodded confirmation. 'There were any number of ways you could find out the truth of what happened, and in a way I would rather you didn't, and I couldn't keep a watch on all of them. There was also the risk that once you were aware of the truth that you—' he broke off, shaking his head frustratedly '—that you were going to hate me for not telling you sooner,' he concluded heavily.

Skye could only stare at him with wide, bewildered eyes, hardly able to believe the lengths he had gone to in order to shield her from the truth. Not sure yet how she felt towards him for having done so...

At the same time, Falkner was so positive of the truth in what he was saying that there was no way she could continue to disbelieve that he at least thought he was telling her the truth. But there was no way she could really believe her uncle Seamus had done the things Falkner was accusing him of—was there?

She and her father had moved back to Ireland over twenty-three years ago to take up residence with her grandfather and her uncle Seamus in the family home, Skye becoming the cherished child of all three men; there was no way she could now believe that her uncle Seamus, the man who had been like a second father to her all these years, was guilty of embezzlement and fraud!

Any more than she had ever believed her father was guilty of it...

Skye sat down heavily in the nearest chair, very much afraid that if she didn't do so she might fall down. 'Those things can't be true about Uncle Seamus, Falkner,' she muttered breathlessly, shaking her head in denial. 'There has to have been some dreadful mistake!'

Falkner looked grim, his hands once again thrust into his trouser pockets. 'Skye, your uncle, unable to live with his own conscience after your father's sudden and unexpected death, was the one to contact the police and confess to them what he had done.'

'But why?' she cried emotionally. 'Why would he ever have done those things?' She blinked as sudden tears clouded her vision.

Falkner drew in a ragged breath. 'I asked him those same questions when I saw him last weekend,' he told her quietly. 'He was the elder brother of the two, I believe?'

Skye looked startled. 'Yes, yes, he was. But he had no interest in the day-to-day business of running a company, so my grandfather—Falkner, you aren't telling me that Uncle Seamus did those things out of spite, because my grandfather left my father in control of O'Hara Whiskey when he died ten years ago?'

Falkner grimaced. 'Basically, yes. In the broader picture—no.'

She shook her head. 'I don't understand.'

He gave a heavy sigh. 'I'm not surprised!' he muttered. 'I had a little trouble understanding myself,' he explained ruefully. 'But it seems that Seamus had no real problem with the status quo, was quite happy to just collect the monthly cheque that was paid to him without his having to do any of the work—until he married. Then it became a problem.'

A small light of comprehension began to appear in the darkness that had enveloped Skye. Her aunt Shanna hadn't been an easy woman to live with, liked to live the luxurious life without having to put too much effort into achieving it.

'Apparently Seamus and Shanna, while resident in Dublin, were living way above their means,' Falkner continued hardly. 'It appears that Shanna had assumed that, as the eldest brother, Seamus actually was O'Hara Whiskey, and she wasn't at all pleased when she found out that it wasn't that way at all, began taunting Seamus about being subservient to his little brother, things like that. The only way round the problem, according to Seamus, was simply to help himself to profits from O'Hara Whiskey.' His mouth twisted distastefully.

Skye blinked. 'But—but how could he do that without my father knowing about it?' She shook her head. 'I can't see how—'

'Your father did know, Skye,' Falkner put in softly.

She raised startled eyes to his. Was Falkner saying that her father had known all the time who was responsible for O'Hara Whiskey's downfall? He couldn't be!

'Connor knew, Skye,' Falkner assured her firmly. 'And I should have guessed…!' He shook his head self-disgustedly. 'I realized several months ago that Connor was keeping something back, protecting someone, but until last weekend I had no idea what or who it was! Your father knew, Skye; I'm sure of it.'

Skye thought back to her uncle Seamus's hurried retreat from Dublin two years ago to the family country estate, of Aunt Shanna's obvious dissatisfaction with the arrangement, of Uncle Seamus's determination, despite his own obvious restlessness, that they would remain there.

Because her father had demanded that he do so after finding out what Seamus had been doing…?

The things Falkner was telling her now certainly put a completely different context on her uncle's move!

Her uncle Seamus had been so angry when Aunt Shanna, unable to stand living in the country any longer, had left him to go back to Dublin, his drinking bouts becoming more frequent, the rows he'd had with his brother often becoming physical as well as verbal.

Skye swallowed hard, feeling sick at the thought of exactly why her uncle had been so angry. 'My father did know,' she confirmed with certainty. 'All this time he knew…!' She groaned, once again burying her face in her hands for the fool she had been.

'Skye—'

Her head snapped up, her eyes flashing a warning Falkner would be very stupid to ignore. He came to a halt inches away from her.

'Don't touch me!' she grated harshly. 'Don't even come near me,' she added coldly. 'I can understand the reasoning behind my father's silence—after all, no matter what his faults, Seamus is his brother. But you— ! How dare you have kept all this from me for the last week?' she demanded furiously, having now decided exactly how she felt about his behaviour this last couple of weeks! 'By what magisterial right did you dare to do the things you've done, go to the lengths that you did, in order to keep me in ignorance of the truth?' Her eyes glittered dangerously.

Falkner frowned. 'Skye, at the moment you're hurt and angry, not a good combination with which to make any sort of considered judgement—'

'Oh, you're right about the angry part, Falkner.' She stood up, her cheeks flushed with fury. 'As to my judgement—I'll make my own mind up about that, thank you very much!' She gave a derisive laugh. 'Do you know, until a short time ago I was feeling utterly bereft, had no idea what I was going to do, or where I was going to go. And then you confused me even more by asking me to marry you,' she recalled scathingly. 'I'm still unsure about what I'm going to do, and where I'm going,' she bit out hardly, 'but one thing I do know—I wouldn't marry you if you—'

'Were the last man on earth?' Falkner finished gratingly. 'Not very original, Skye,' he mocked hardly.

Her eyes flashed deeply blue. 'I was actually going to say if you came gift-wrapped,' she told him scornfully, her hands clenched into fists at her sides. 'Am I to take it, from what you said earlier, that the estate in Ireland, along with everything else, will be sold in an effort to repay the stock-holders the money my uncle cheated them of?' She looked at him with narrowed eyes.

'Yes,' Falkner confirmed heavily.

Skye shook her head disbelievingly. 'You really have to be the most arrogant man I have ever had the misfortune to meet! How dare you ask me to marry you, as if I'm some sort of homeless charity case—?'

'That isn't the reason I asked you to marry me, Skye—'

'Of course it is,' she cut in distastefully, uncaring of the anger that now darkened Falkner's grimly set features. 'What do you think I am, Falkner?' she scoffed. 'Did you really think I would just meekly sit here and listen to all you have to say, and then gratefully accept your marriage proposal? Because if you did—'

'I didn't expect anything about your reaction to be meek,' he assured her humourlessly.

At this precise moment Skye wanted to scream and

shout, to hit something—or someone!—but she wasn't going to do any of those things. She wouldn't give Falkner the satisfaction!

'Then you weren't disappointed, were you?' she bit out forcefully. 'I'm going upstairs to pack my things now. In the circumstances, would it be too much to ask you to call a taxi for me?'

His mouth twisted wryly. 'Can I take it that's a definite no to my marriage proposal?'

Skye opened her mouth to give him a scathing reply, and then thought better of it; she had to get out of here before she totally lost it and said several things she might later—not regret, exactly, but certainly wish unsaid!

'Just call me a taxi, please, Falkner,' she told him wearily as she walked heavily towards the door.

He frowned. 'But where are you going?'

She turned sharply on her heels. 'Believe it or not, Falkner, and despite what you may have thought to the contrary, I do have other friends besides you! In fact, you come way down the list of people I would ever ask—'

'Don't add insult to injury, Skye,' he warned tautly, that nerve once again pulsing in his tightly clenched jaw. 'Whatever you may think of me now, I can assure you that I did act out of friendship.'

'For my father.' She nodded.

'And you,' he assured her huskily.

Skye gave a decisive shake of her head. 'We aren't friends, Falkner,' she bit out derisively. 'Friends don't lie to each other,' she added.

He gave a shake of his head. 'I have never lied to you, Skye,' he rasped. 'Omitted to tell the truth, perhaps,' he allowed dryly. 'But I didn't lie.'

'That's pure semantics, Falkner, and you know it!' She shook her head disgustedly.

He gave a heavy sigh. 'Maybe. If you leave now, what are you going to do about Storm?'

She had completely forgotten about the stallion in her need to get away from Falkner!

Her mouth twisted. 'As you were arrogant enough to bring him here in the first place I suggest you continue to look after him until I can make alternative arrangements!' Although quite what they were going to be, or when, she had no idea.

She really didn't have any definite place to go once she had left here, just knew that she could no longer stay here, living on what amounted to Falkner's charity.

He nodded abruptly. 'I'll drive you wherever you want to go.'

'Thanks—but no, thanks!' Skye snapped, still angry, but knowing that reaction to the things Falkner had just told her was soon going to set in—and then she was going to fall apart! She did not want to do that anywhere near Falkner.

'Skye—'

'Oh, never mind, Falkner, I'll call my own taxi,' she told him impatiently. 'Or walk. Either way, I'm getting out of here!' she assured him purposefully.

'Don't bother—I'll call the damned taxi!' he grated harshly, his expression grim, eyes a cold, icy blue, hands clenched at his sides—as if he were barely restraining himself from wringing her neck!

Skye left the room without another word, running up the stairs to the bedroom she had been using during her stay. And all the time the words, How dare he? How dare he? were ringing in her ears.

She slammed the bedroom door behind her, moving determinedly about the room to throw her few belongings haphazardly back into her suitcase, allowing no time for thought—there would be plenty of time for that once she was safely away from here.

Who would ever have guessed that only hours ago she had buried her beloved father—?

No!

She couldn't think of that now either, had to concentrate on getting away from here, away from Falkner, without breaking down. Once she had done that—

She moved to the window as she heard a car out on the driveway, her mouth tightening as she saw Falkner approach the taxi to talk briefly to the driver, her heart contracting painfully as his limp seemed more pronounced than usual.

She turned away from the window, determined to remain unaffected by Falkner's obvious weariness. If she resented his charity, then she knew Falkner would welcome her pity even less.

He was waiting in the hallway as Skye came down the stairs, his expression no less grim, although his anger seemed to have faded as he looked at her with guarded eyes. 'You shouldn't have carried that down the stairs.' He nodded at the suitcase she had put down in the hallway.

Her mouth twisted. 'Falkner, at this precise moment my ribs are the least of my problems!' In fact, she hadn't even given her broken ribs a thought the last half an hour, let alone felt any pain from them, sheer anger her main impetus!

Falkner sighed. 'I really wish you would reconsider, Skye,' he murmured huskily.

She eyed him scathingly. 'Your insulting marriage proposal? Or leaving?'

His mouth tightened. 'Leaving, of course,' he rasped.

Skye gave a humourless smile. 'I have no intention of reconsidering anything you've said to me today—least of all my leaving. In fact, I can't wait to get away,' she added insultingly. 'I'll be in touch concerning Storm.' She frowned, her gaze suddenly pained as something else occurred to her. 'Does he have to be sold as well?'

His head rose challengingly. 'Storm is yours.'

Which probably meant that Falkner had made sure the stallion would remain hers, probably by buying him himself. She didn't know how, or when, but she would make sure she paid him back every penny he had paid to buy Storm for her.

She gave a terse inclination of her head now. 'Thank you.'

Falkner's mouth twisted ruefully. 'That must have hurt!'

'You have no idea!' she told him scathingly, bending down to pick up her suitcase.

'I've already instructed the taxi driver to leave by the back entrance—'

'Then I'll just have to uninstruct him, won't I?' she came back tartly as she straightened.

'The reporters will still be at the main entrance,' he reasoned impatiently.

'I don't care!' Skye glared at him. 'My hiding days are over, Falkner,' she snapped decisively.

He shook his head. 'That isn't a good idea, Skye—'

'I have nothing to hide, Falkner,' she bit out determinedly.

'Do you really think they care?' he said impatiently. 'Skye, at the moment, you're news—'

'And will remain so while I continue to give the appearance I do have something to hide.' She shook her head. 'They can't touch me now. None of you can,' she added firmly.

Falkner drew in a hissing breath at her deliberate insult. 'If you should need me—'

'I won't,' she dismissed derisively; she would make sure that she didn't need Falkner ever again.

The fact that she loved him, still, was just something that she would have to live with. She had lived with it for six years already, what did the rest of her life matter?

'I'll carry that out for you.' He reached to take the suitcase from her hand.

Skye moved sharply away from him. 'I can manage. Goodbye, Falkner,' she told him firmly, walking to the door. 'I'll be in touch as soon as I can concerning Storm.'

'He's perfectly okay where he is,' he grated.

She turned briefly. 'I would prefer he was with me.'

Falkner's mouth tightened. 'Whatever,' he sighed defeatedly.

Skye's last sight of him was in the mirror of the taxi as they drove down the driveway.

He stood alone on the gravel outside the house, a tall, solitary figure, his face set in grim lines as he watched the taxi slowly disappear…

CHAPTER EIGHT

'HEAR me out, Skye, before you close the door in my face!' Belinda said quickly—obviously realizing there was a possibility that Skye would do exactly that.

Opening her hotel door to find Belinda Chapman standing in the hallway outside was the very last thing Skye had been expecting; she had thought it was the landlady with the extra towels she had promised to bring up to her.

As it happened, Skye hadn't gone very far in the taxi the day before, just into the local town, taking a room at the inn/hotel in the square there, having remembered seeing it when she went shopping with Falkner. Also having decided that it didn't really matter where she went at the moment, that here was as good a place as any to think about her immediate future. Besides, she didn't have any money to waste on luxuries, and the nightly rate at this small hotel was much cheaper than a London hotel ever would have been!

Her mouth tightened as she looked at the older woman. 'If Falkner sent you—'

'He didn't,' Belinda assured her with a grimace. 'In fact, his last instructions to me were to stay well away from you!'

'But…?' Skye raised pointedly questioning brows.

The other woman shrugged. 'I never was too good at doing what I was told!'

Skye gave a rueful smile; neither was she! Besides, she liked Belinda.

She stepped back. 'You had better come in,' she invited grudgingly; after all, it wasn't Belinda's fault that she had an arrogantly interfering brother.

'Thanks.' Belinda stepped inside the room, looking about her interestedly at the small but elegantly furnished room and its adjoining bathroom. 'This place is really quite nice, isn't it?' she allowed admiringly.

'I think so.' Skye nodded, still eyeing her warily. Just because Falkner hadn't asked his sister to come here didn't mean she was pleased by Belinda's visit. Besides… 'How did you know I was staying here?' She frowned.

'Ah.' The other woman grimaced. 'Well, I could say that it's a small town. Or that my cleaning lady also cleans here—which she does, by the way,' Belinda added lightly, 'that she recognized you and mentioned the fact to me. Or—'

'The truth will do, Belinda,' Skye told her wryly, moving to fill the kettle in order to make them both a cup of coffee.

'Falkner asked the taxi driver to let him know where he took you yesterday,' Belinda admitted evenly. 'Now I know how that must sound, Skye.' She rushed into speech as Skye's face darkened angrily as she turned from making the coffee.

'It *sounds* exactly like Falkner!' she corrected exasperatedly; he had probably been doing exactly that yesterday when she'd looked down on the driveway and seen him chatting to the taxi driver.

'Yes, it does,' Belinda acknowledged ruefully. 'But he's genuinely concerned about you, Skye—'

'Please don't take offence at this, Belinda,' she cut in coldly, 'but the least I hear about your arrogant brother at the moment, the better I'll like it!'

Belinda sighed. 'I can understand that. I did try to warn him…' She shrugged ruefully.

'I heard you.' Skye nodded. 'I didn't mean to eavesdrop, but I couldn't help overhearing your conversation with Falkner the day the children came to tea,' she explained at Belinda's questioning look. 'Sugar?' She held up the cup of coffee she had just made.

'I'm on a diet.' Belinda shook her head. 'I'm always on a diet since I had the children,' she added with a grimace as she took the cup of coffee. 'Actually, it's because of the children I'm here—well, not just because of the children, of course, but—'

'Belinda, why don't you just spit it out, hmm?' Skye encouraged dryly as she sat in the chair opposite.

Belinda nodded. 'It's the twins' birthday party tomorrow.'

'I remember.' Once again Skye was on her guard.

Belinda gave another nod. 'Well, they were really disappointed they couldn't come to dinner with us when we came to you and Falkner on Thursday evening, so to placate them at the time I told them you would be at their barbecue tomorrow. Believing, of course, at the time, that you would be,' she added hastily. 'They are very upset with their uncle Fork for letting you leave before their party.'

Skye's brows rose. 'I don't think it was actually a case of him having "let" me do anything.' Although she could imagine that having the twins annoyed with him wasn't something Falkner was accustomed to; he was more used to their adoration.

'No, well, I did try to tell them that.' Belinda sighed. 'But children don't understand these things. Especially almost-six-year-olds!' she added with feeling.

Skye had spent the last twenty-four hours at this hotel coming to terms with her changed circumstances.

The very first thing she had done was to speak to her uncle in Ireland, to assure him of her continued love and support for him; that was something, after due consideration, she knew her father would have wanted. Her offer to return to Ireland to be with him was refused, but she promised Uncle Seamus that when the time came she would return to Ireland for his trial.

The second thing she had done was to check exactly what funds she still had available to her; she had received all her father's personal effects at the hospital, finding five hundred pounds in his wallet. Surely that, if nothing else, was still legally hers…?

The third thing she had done, knowing that five hundred pounds wouldn't last for very long, was to look at her options for employment, taking into account exactly what she was qualified for.

She had been her father's personal assistant since the age of eighteen, both at O'Hara Whiskey, and at the stables he ran on the estate. She had finally decided, with her uncle Seamus's trial hanging over her head, that she couldn't seriously expect anyone to take her on as their PA, and that she probably stood more chance of finding a job at the latter rather than the former.

And what better place to find that sort of job than here, in the heart of horse-racing country, with over a dozen stables in the vicinity listed in the local telephone directory? In fact, she had already telephoned a couple of them and ascertained that they had vacancies for stable-lads/lasses, was going over tomorrow morning to meet with the stable managers. Besides, living and working at a stable, there was every chance she might be allowed to take Storm with her…

In fact, the only drawback she had seen to these possibilities was Falkner's close proximity.

But even that didn't have to be a problem, she had decided; she had more than made her feelings clear to Falkner about the two of them meeting again. Besides, she had reasoned—before Belinda's visit today had told her the contrary—Falkner didn't even have to know she was still in the area; she very much doubted, as a lowly stable-hand, she would ever run into him socially.

Except, if she wasn't mistaken, Belinda now seemed to be asking her to do exactly that.

'I know it's a lot to ask, Skye.' The other woman easily sensed her misgivings. 'But if I promise to do everything in my power to keep you and Falkner apart…?'

Skye gave her a pitying look. 'And what chance do you think you have of making that happen if Falkner should decide otherwise?' But after the way they had parted yesterday, that wasn't very likely. Although she doubted Falkner had confided in his sister concerning his marriage proposal—and its refusal.

Belinda gave a sudden grin. 'I'll give him the job of cooking the barbecue with Charles; that should keep him busy!'

Skye's immediate thought was that Falkner probably shouldn't be on his injured leg for any length of time—and then she chastised herself for even having the thought; nothing Falkner did or said in his life was of any concern to her.

'The twins will be so disappointed if you don't come, Skye,' the other woman encouraged cajolingly.

She gave a husky laugh. 'Does that ploy usually work, Belinda?'

'Usually, yes,' Belinda admitted ruefully.

Why not? After feeling the last two weeks as if everything was running out of her control, Skye felt as if the last twenty-four hours she had actually taken that control of her life back again. She wasn't about to let Falkner, or anyone else for that matter, take that away from her ever again.

But was she ready to see Falkner again quite this soon after telling him exactly what he could do with himself and his idea of helping her...?

The answer to that was definitely yes. She might have grown in confidence these last twenty-four hours—especially if she managed to get a job tomorrow—but she had also gained in maturity this last two weeks, too. A maturity that meant she was more than capable of meeting Falkner tomorrow at the birthday party of his niece and nephew.

Belinda was still looking at her hopefully. And the twins were adorable...

'Okay,' Skye sighed her agreement. 'But if Falkner so much as looks like causing a scene—'

'He won't,' Belinda assured her quickly, standing up to leave, unable to hide the smile of triumph she felt at the successful outcome of her visit. 'It's casual dress, by the way,' she said on her way to the door.

Apart from a couple of business suits Skye had brought with her on this initial business trip with her father, she didn't have any other clothes but casual!

Besides, it was oldest clothes she was going to need if she was working in a stable.

If.

That was the question…

'You're the last person I expected to see here today!'

So much for Belinda's promise—Skye had only arrived five minutes ago, and almost the first person to speak to her was Falkner.

Skye stiffened, taking her time about turning to face him, smiling her thanks to Jemmy for her orange juice as he and Lissa moved excitedly amongst their guests with trays containing glasses of juice.

Because Falkner was taking round a similar tray with the glasses of wine, Skye discovered as she slowly turned around, not seeming to have started on cooking the barbecue yet. Obviously, from his opening remark, Belinda hadn't told him she had persuaded Skye into being here today.

'I had hoped for the same thing,' she answered Falkner coolly now.

His mouth twisted into the semblance of a smile. 'Sorry to disappoint you!'

Skye continued to look at him coldly. 'You aren't sorry at all, Falkner.'

'No,' he allowed evenly, his narrowed gaze searching on her face. 'Are you okay?' he prompted huskily.

She bristled resentfully. 'Why shouldn't I be?'

He shrugged. 'The newspapers yesterday weren't exactly—kind.'

Skye gave a dismissive shrug. 'I've decided not to read newspapers—until they start printing something that is actually news.' In truth, she had seen the story of

her father's funeral in the newspapers yesterday, the un-
flattering photograph of her as she'd left the church on
Friday. 'Are they still camped out at your place?' she
prompted uninterestedly.

Falkner shrugged. 'One or two.'

Skye nodded, knowing very well that in a day or two
she would be old news. Perhaps then everyone could get
on with their lives. In the meantime, she intended
getting on with hers!

'I'm sorry about that.' She grimaced.

'It doesn't matter,' he dismissed. 'Skye—'

'Falkner, it's time you went and helped Charles with
the barbecue.' Belinda arrived briskly on the scene.
'Besides, you aren't doing too well as a wine-waiter!'
She took the tray of drinks from his unresisting hands.

He smiled unrepentantly at his sister. 'It wasn't what
I was trained for.'

'I have yet to see exactly what you were trained for,
Falkner,' Belinda came back archly. 'Why don't you try
your hand at cooking?'

He gave his sister a quizzical look. 'Why do I have
the feeling this is some sort of female conspiracy?'

'Probably because you men always come to that conclusion!' Belinda returned waspishly.

Falkner gave a shake of his head. 'I should have
warned Charles about you before he married you!'

'I did warn him,' Belinda assured him unrepentantly.
'He said he was willing to take the risk.'

Falkner glanced across to where his brother-in-law
was laughing with the twins as they brought out the food
they were going to need to feed the fifty or so guests
who were here for the twins' birthday, the parents
having been invited as well as the children.

'He looks well enough on it,' Falkner murmured ruefully.

Skye had been watching and listening to this interplay between brother and sister with fascination; as an only child, brought up by men, she had never had this sort of verbal exchange in her own life. It looked like fun.

Except that one of the people having that fun was the man she had to hold herself aloof from if she were to survive the next few weeks. The man she loved...!

'You should try it some time, Falkner,' Belinda told her brother challengingly now.

His humour faded, his expression becoming grim. 'I did, remember? It was a disaster. I would be a fool to even contemplate going through that again,' he grated, his gaze icy as it swept dismissively over Skye.

She felt the warmth in her cheeks at this reminder— to her at least!—of his proposal to her two days ago. A proposal she had turned down...

'Are you going to help Charles or not?' Belinda asked pointedly.

'I am,' Falkner bit out abruptly, giving Skye a terse nod. 'Perhaps I'll see you again later,' was his parting shot.

Not if she saw him first, was her own, inward, answer to that! From the derisive smile that curved Falkner's mouth as he strolled across to join his brother-in-law, it was a thought he was perfectly attuned to!

'Whew.' Belinda let out a relieved sigh at her brother's departure. 'I'm really sorry about that, Skye; one minute you were chatting happily to the twins, the next Falkner was here!' She shook her head. 'I got over here as quickly as I could.'

Skye gave a husky laugh at the other woman's obvious panic. 'Don't worry about it, Belinda; I really am quite capable of dealing with Falkner,' she assured her softly. And knowing that she actually was...

'I know, but I promised.' Belinda grimaced. 'The twins love the toys you brought for them, by the way.'

Skye smiled warmly. 'They're very welcome.' To buy the presents for the twins had taken a big chunk out of the money she had at her disposal, but there was no way she was going to come here today without giving them something.

Belinda glanced across to where Falkner and Charles were busy putting food on the barbecue. 'I know I ragged him unmercifully just now, but Falkner really has had a rough time this last few years, emotionally as well as physically,' she added with an affectionate grimace.

Skye's brows lowered in a heavy frown. 'If you're trying to make me feel guilty—'

'Oh, but I'm not,' the older woman instantly assured her. 'I was just—well, yes, I suppose it could appear that way,' she allowed with a rueful wrinkling of her nose. 'It's just—Falkner and I have always been close, and— I don't like to see him unhappy.'

Skye gave a dismissive shake of her head. 'If he's unhappy then it isn't because of me,' she said with certainty. 'In fact, he should be pleased to have me out of his hair.'

'He doesn't look very pleased.' Belinda laughed dryly.

No, Skye inwardly agreed after a brief glimpse at Falkner; if anything he looked grimly determined as he helped Charles.

'He'll get used to it,' Skye dismissed as she turned away. 'Tell me who some of your other guests are,' she invited lightly.

It was obvious, over the next few minutes, as Belinda

was greeted by some of those other guests, that the Chapman family were very well liked in the area, Belinda finally having to excuse herself as she was called over to organize the order of the food being cooked on the barbecue.

There were about fifty people altogether, and if any of them recognized Skye from the photograph in the newspaper yesterday, they were too polite to say so. In fact, an hour later, Skye was having such a good time that she had almost forgotten Falkner's brooding presence over by the barbecue.

Almost…

It would be impossible to forget him altogether, especially as every time she glanced his way that brooding gaze was focused on her. Oh, Falkner gave the barbecue his attention occasionally, but for the main part he watched Skye as she laughed and chatted with several of the other guests, the scowl on his face speaking of his impatience with his own preoccupation.

'Selina…?'

Skye frowned as she turned to face the man who had spoken questioningly behind her, smiling enquiringly as she found herself looking at a tall, pleasant-faced man of about thirty. Although that face was slightly pale now as he stared at her disbelievingly.

'No.' He spoke again, slowly. 'It isn't, is it? For a minute there I really thought—' He shook his head, making an effort to pull himself together. 'I'm sorry, I'm being extremely rude.' He attempted a smile. 'It was just that you reminded me of someone else for a moment.'

Someone 'else' called Selina…

Selina Harrington?

'That's okay,' Skye told him lightly; at least he hadn't

recognized her as the Skye O'Hara whose photograph had appeared in the newspapers yesterday! 'You aren't the first person to make that mistake,' she assured him.

No, he wasn't, was he...?

Could this perhaps be the reason for Falkner's sudden marriage proposal to her on Friday? Because she was apparently a look-alike for his ex-wife...?

CHAPTER NINE

'I'M SORRY, I should have introduced myself.' The young man was recovering quickly from his earlier mistake concerning her identity, his smile openly friendly now, the colour having returned to his cheeks. 'Paul Barclay.' He held out his hand to her. 'I'm one of the many local vets.'

'Skye,' she returned noncommittally as she briefly shook his hand. 'Pleased to meet you.'

'And you.' He nodded, a tall, slender man, with unruly blond hair that he habitually brushed from his forehead, only to have it fall straight back again. 'Are you a friend of the family?'

She shrugged. 'I do know the whole family, yes, but I'm here primarily at the twins' invitation.' She had no idea what she and Falkner were—but it certainly wasn't friends!

'Belinda and Charles are a great couple, aren't they?' Paul nodded.

'I—we're quite new acquaintances, but, yes, I find them very likeable,' Skye answered carefully. 'And the twins are adorable,' she added without hesitation.

'I'm called in occasionally to look at the family dog,' Paul explained his own presence here.

Skye had seen the Golden Labrador wandering amongst the guests, its tail wagging happily. 'I don't think he's going to need your assistance today.' Skye smiled.

'No.' Paul returned her smile, his brown gaze warmly admiring as he looked at her. 'I believe Belinda has announced that the food is ready; shall we wander over and get some?'

Apart from the fact that he had initially mistaken her for Falkner's ex-wife, Paul Barclay seemed pleasant enough; Belinda had made the same mistake on the day the two of them had been introduced, and it hadn't affected her liking for the other woman. Besides, she would rather not be on her own when she went for her food; Falkner was still cooking on the barbecue!

'That sounds lovely,' Skye accepted, putting down her empty glass on one of the tables that had been placed outside.

'Great!' Paul gave a boyish smile.

He was thirty-three and a bachelor, Skye learnt as they strolled over to the laden tables, had lived in the area for four years, and found it very much to his liking.

'Even more so now,' he added with an obviously warm glance in Skye's direction.

Skye wasn't exactly sure she wanted this man to like her too much; she was going to be living in the area for a while, and as things stood it probably wasn't a good idea to clutter her life with any complications. Besides, this man had initially thought she was Selina Harrington...

Skye gave him a sideways glance. 'Were you a friend of Selina Harrington's?' she asked casually, remembering the genuine pleasure in Paul's voice when he had thought she was the other woman. If he had been a friend of the other woman's, then he was the first person Skye had met who admitted to being so!

His face flushed as he gave a dismissive shrug. 'I knew her quite well, yes.'

Not quite an admission, after all, Skye mused, wondering exactly what sort of 'friends' Paul and Selina had been.

'Mmm, this foods looks delicious!' she enthused as they arrived at the tables laden with salads and pastas as well as the meats cooked on the barbecue.

'I'm a bachelor; any food that someone else has prepared looks wonderful to me!' Paul answered self-derisively as he handed her a plate before taking one for himself. 'My usual Sunday evening meal is beans on toast!'

Skye laughed. As she was meant to do, she was sure, confirming that Paul hadn't welcomed her questioning about his friendship with Selina Harrington.

Oh, well, it was really none of her business, was it? After all, Selina had divorced Falkner amid accusations of another woman, not the other way around.

'What do you think you're doing?'

Skye stiffened, Paul Barclay having moved some way ahead of her as she easily recognized Falkner's voice saying those words in her ear.

She turned to him frowningly, that frown deepening as she saw the scowl on his face. 'I'm getting myself some food, what does it look like I'm doing?' she answered irritably.

Falkner's gaze narrowed at her sarcasm. 'You and Paul Barclay seem to be very friendly,' he rasped.

Skye glanced across to where the other man was now chatting easily to Charles. 'He seems very nice.'

She shrugged dismissively; after all, the other man had been friendly and nice.

Falkner's jaw clenched. 'You're far from the first woman in the area to think so!'

Was he referring to Selina, his ex-wife? Or did he mean someone else?

She shrugged. 'Why not? He's probably considered a very eligible bachelor.'

'Oh, very,' Falkner acknowledged scathingly. 'Don't you have enough complications in your life already without bringing some man into it?'

The fact that she had already come to that conclusion herself didn't mean that she appreciated Falkner actually saying it!

Her mouth tightened. 'Maybe "some man" in my life is exactly what I need to uncomplicate it,' she snapped resentfully. 'With the exception of you, of course!' she added derisively, eyes brightly blue in her anger.

Falkner drew in a harsh breath. 'Why with the exception of me?' he challenged hardly.

Skye gave a humourless laugh. 'Probably because you are the most complicated man I have ever met!'

He gave a perplexed frown. 'What's so complicated about me?'

She gave a derisive shake of her head. 'There simply isn't enough time right now to go into all that!'

He raised dark brows. 'Have dinner with me tomorrow evening, we can discuss it then, try to make me a little less "complicated",' he added dryly.

Skye's eyes widened at the invitation. Was Falkner actually asking her out on a date? Or did he just mean she was invited back to the house for dinner?

He was also, by asking to see her tomorrow evening

at all, confirming that he was well aware of the fact that she was staying at the hotel in town!

Her mouth tightened at the thought of the arrogant way he had obtained that information from the taxi driver.

'There's a rather nice French restaurant on the edge of town,' Falkner continued firmly—as if he had sensed she was about to turn down his invitation.

He was asking her out on a date. Incredible! Six months ago she would have been ecstatic at the invitation, even three weeks ago she would have felt the same way, but after the events of the last two weeks she could only view the invitation with suspicion.

'If I book a table at Francois for eight o'clock, I could call for you at the hotel at seven-thirty—'

'No, you couldn't,' Skye cut in determinedly.

His eyes narrowed. 'Why couldn't I?'

'For one thing, I haven't accepted your invitation to dinner,' she told him exasperatedly.

'And for a second thing…?' he prompted slowly.

She was no longer staying at the hotel, had booked out an hour or so before coming to the birthday party!

She had been successful at her first job interview this morning, the position as stable-girl including purpose-built accommodation close to the stables themselves. The actual wages for the job, as she had suspected, weren't very high, but the inclusion of the accommodation, relieving her of the need to pay a hotel bill, more than made up for that.

But she didn't want to tell Falkner about her new job, not what it was, or where she was living…

For the first time in her life she was on her own, having to make her own way, and even if she did say so herself she wasn't doing too bad a job of it so far. She had found employment, and accommodation, and the stable manager was quite happy for her to bring Storm with her. As long as she looked after him and paid towards his keep. Which she was quite happy to do.

'The "one thing" is quite sufficient reason for the moment,' she told Falkner sharply. 'Exactly why are you inviting me out to dinner, Falkner?' she prompted dryly; if it had anything to do with the fact that she had struck up a conversation with Paul Barclay, then he could just forget it!

He shrugged broad shoulders. 'It seems like a neighbourly thing to do.'

'Neighbourly!' Skye echoed incredulously. 'Falkner, you live at least three miles out of town!'

'More like four,' he acknowledged dryly. 'But distance doesn't mean the same thing here in the country.'

No, it probably didn't, she accepted, knowing that it was pretty much the same in Ireland. But even so…

'Skye, Friday wasn't the time to go into this, but there are still some things we have to discuss,' Falkner continued determinedly, glancing past Skye to where he could see Paul Barclay making his way back to them.

'Such as?' she challenged, also aware of the other man's approach—and the increase in Falkner's tension. Because of the other man…? She had no idea.

Just as she had no idea whether or not she should accept Falkner's dinner invitation. Part of her said, having got away once, that she should stay well away from him. But another part of her, the part that loved him so much it was torture just talking to him like this, wanted so desperately to say yes!

His mouth twisted mockingly. '"There simply isn't enough time"—or privacy!—"right now to go into all that".' He dryly quoted her own earlier answer to him back at her, at the same time glancing pointedly towards the rapidly approaching Paul Barclay. 'Oh, come on, Skye, it's only dinner, for goodness' sake,' he added impatiently as she still hesitated.

It might only be dinner to him, but to Skye it was reopening that door she had only recently slammed in his face.

Falkner bent his head, his mouth only inches from her ear now. 'How about if I promise not to even mention the word marriage?' he prompted softly.

Skye moved back sharply, her head raised challengingly. 'Don't even think about it,' she snapped impatiently. 'Oh, okay, Falkner, dinner tomorrow evening. But I'll make my own way to the restaurant,' she added firmly, irritated as his face was lit by triumph at her acceptance.

Some of that triumph faded from his face. 'And just how do you intend doing that? The last I heard, you didn't have a car,' he prompted frowningly.

She still didn't have one, but she did have the use of one; the manager at the stable had told her there were a couple of old Land Rovers that the stable-hands could use if need be. It might not be the best way of avoiding having Falkner call and collect her, but for the moment she didn't want him to know where she was staying.

But his mention of her not having a car had reminded Skye of what had happened two weeks ago, the Mercedes her father had hired for their stay in England a complete write-off in the accident.

Falkner's expression darkened as he must have seen that knowledge in her suddenly bereft expression. 'Damn it, Skye, I didn't mean to—'

'Here you are, Skye.' Paul Barclay had finally

reached them, a laden plate held in one hand. 'You're missing out on all the food,' he told her lightly. 'Falkner,' he greeted, his glance guarded as he turned to look at the other man.

Or was that just Skye's imagination? Probably not, if Falkner's attitude earlier to the other man was anything to go by.

'Barclay,' he returned distantly. 'I'll see you for dinner tomorrow evening, then, Skye,' he added briskly, giving Paul Barclay a curt nod before striding back, with that slightly lopsided gait he had adopted since his riding accident, to join Charles at the barbecue.

There was an awkward silence after his departure. One deliberately created by Falkner by his parting remark, Skye guessed as she glared across at him impatiently.

'I had no idea you and Falkner were such good friends.' Paul Barclay spoke lightly at her side.

A forced lightness, Skye easily guessed from his suddenly strained expression, giving credence to her earlier guess of the two men not liking each other very much. Because of Selina Harrington? She wondered once again. Possibly, but she had no intention of asking Paul Barclay about that, and she doubted very much that Falkner would confide that information to her!

'We're acquaintances,' she corrected firmly. 'I did tell you that I know the family,' she reminded lightly.

'So you did,' Paul accepted with a rueful smile. 'I'm sure Belinda will make the two of you a great meal tomorrow evening; she's a wonderful cook!'

She was sure Belinda was a good cook; the other woman seemed more than capable at most things. She just wouldn't be cooking for Falkner and Skye tomorrow evening!

She eyed Paul teasingly. 'Is it still true that the way to a man's heart is through his stomach?'

'It is to a bachelor of thirty-three!' he returned self-derisively.

Skye gave a rueful shake of her head. 'What a pity I never got beyond the bacon-and-egg stage!'

Paul's eyes glowed appreciatively. 'I'm sure it's not too late to learn!'

Skye sobered; it really wouldn't do to encourage this man when she had no real interest in him other than the fact he appeared to be a nice man. Over the years, she had discovered there were a lot of nice men in the world, but when she was already in love with one of them, there was absolutely no point in flirting with any others. And flirting with Falkner was definitely out of the question!

'Sadly I have no interest in learning,' she told Paul briskly. 'But as I am rather hungry, I think I'll take your advice and help myself to some food.'

Unfortunately, Paul didn't take this as the hint it had been for him to leave her side. Instead he accompanied her over to the table once she had her food, sitting down with her as she deliberately turned their conversation to more general things concerning the area.

Paul proved to be quite an amusing companion as he related some of the funnier cases he had been called to deal with.

But it was nevertheless impossible for Skye to relax in his company, all the time aware as Paul chatted lightly of Falkner's brooding gaze fixed on them in total disapproval!

CHAPTER TEN

'WHAT on earth have you been doing with yourself?'

Skye scowled impatiently at Falkner, having just joined him at the table he had reserved at Francois.

She had been trying so hard not to let him see how stiffly she was moving, her hours spent in the saddle today having done absolutely nothing for her two broken ribs. From his opening remark, she might just as well have saved herself the trouble of the hot bath and the pain-killers she had taken before coming out, too!

She eased herself gingerly down into the chair Falkner had stood up to hold back for her, grateful when he moved away to sit down in his own chair opposite.

'Well?' he rasped at her continued silence.

'Good evening to you too, Falkner,' she returned with obvious sarcasm. 'May I say how lovely you're looking this evening?' she added pointedly.

Falkner looked unimpressed. 'You do look lovely. You always do. But you're also moving as if someone has driven over you with a steamroller!'

The glow of pleasure Skye had felt at his first comments was easily wiped out by the one that followed! 'Thanks.' She grimaced, inwardly acknowledging that he did indeed look wonderful this evening, his dark suit obviously expensively tailored, the blue of his shirt an exact match for the colour of his eyes.

'You're welcome,' he bit out dryly, still looking at her with narrowed eyes. 'So what have you been doing?'

Dogged came to mind, Skye acknowledged irritatedly. 'This and that,' she dismissed lightly. 'Do you think I might have a sparkling water?'

'I'll order some wine.'

'I'm driving,' Skye refused. 'The sparkling water will be fine.'

Falkner ordered two sparkling waters from a passing waiter, before turning back to her. 'You're driving?' he repeated, brows raised. 'You've bought yourself a car since we spoke yesterday?'

'Not exactly,' she avoided; the Land Rover she had borrowed for the evening left a lot to be desired in the line of comfort, Skye had discovered earlier, having to put a blanket on the front seat before she could sit in it in her black dress, the vehicle also seeming to feel every bump and pothole in the road on the drive here. 'But I do have transport,' she added unhelpfully. 'I believe you said there are some things we still need to discuss…?'

His mouth twisted derisively. 'Is it okay with you if we order our food first?'

Skye felt as if she had just received a slap on the wrist. A light one, but still a slap.

'Fine.' She picked up the menu, placing it in front of her as she looked at the food listed there.

Blast the man. He always seemed to have a way of taking control of any situation, and turning it to his advantage. Well, she hadn't been at all sure about having dinner with him this evening as it was, so he had better have a genuine reason for getting her here!

'You checked out of the hotel.' Falkner spoke as soon as they had ordered their food, pâté and chicken for Skye, soup and steak for Falkner.

Skye gave him a sharp look. 'And how would you know that?'

He shrugged unconcernedly. 'I telephoned you there earlier today, Margaret said you checked out yesterday.'

Yes, she had, and the accommodation at the stables might not be quite as luxurious as the hotel—it was also unheated, she had discovered last night—but at least it went free with her new job. Beggars couldn't be choosers, she had decided ruefully as she'd pulled on a pair of socks before getting into bed.

'So?' she returned lightly.

'So you checked out of the hotel,' Falkner repeated pointedly.

'What is your point, Falkner?' Skye prompted impatiently.

'My point is that you are obviously still staying in the area,' he bit out forcefully.

'And?' Really, it was none of Falkner's business that she had booked out of the hotel, or where she was staying now!

He gave a heavy sigh. 'Skye, unless it's escaped your notice, this is a pretty tight-knit community. Sooner or later someone is going to tell me where you're staying now, so you may as well give me the information yourself!'

'And deprive you of the pleasure of listening to gossip?' she taunted.

His eyes flashed warningly. 'I never listen to gossip, Skye—but Belinda does,' he added dryly. 'And you can be sure that my little sister will then pass the information on to me—whether I want to know or not!'

'Then why don't you just wait and see how long it takes for that little piece of information to reach you?' Skye returned sweetly.

'Skye—'

'I think the more important point here, Falkner, is why you telephoned me earlier today at all,' she cut in firmly. 'Don't you?'

He looked as if he would like to argue the point, but, as their first course arrived at that moment, he waited until they were alone again before speaking. 'Your father's lawyer contacted me again this morning; he would like to see us as soon as convenient,' he told her with obvious reluctance.

Rightly so. Because there could only be one reason her father's lawyer would need to see her so urgently— for the reading of the will that had been cancelled on Friday. Just the mention of it was enough to put a complete dampener on the evening. As if it hadn't been tense enough already!

To delay the moment of truth even further Skye picked up some Melba toast and began to eat her pâté. Although her appetite suddenly seemed to have deserted her...

Which was a pity. Because, apart from the fact that she ached in every bone in her body after a gruelling day's work, she had actually felt as if her new job was a positive move forward; the mention of the lawyer took her back into the nightmare.

'I don't see why he needs to see me at all,' Skye finally dismissed hardly. 'My father put every bit of money he had into paying off the creditors of O'Hara Whiskey. He had no money left when he—when he died.'

'The company had no money,' Falkner corrected softly.

'Same thing,' Skye muttered.

'Not really.' He shook his head. 'Although up to a point, you're correct.'

Her eyes narrowed. 'And which "point" would that be?'

'Skye, several years ago—before all this trouble with your uncle Seamus blew up in his face,' he added hardly, 'your father went in with me on several financial ventures. To our mutual benefit.'

'He did?' she said slowly; her father had never mentioned these financial ventures to her…

'He did.' Falkner nodded firmly.

She shrugged. 'Even if that's true…' and she wasn't a hundred-per-cent certain that she believed it was, suspected this might be another attempt at some sort of misguided charity on Falkner's part—although she hadn't quite worked out what it could be yet '…how can you be sure he didn't reinvest that money into O'Hara Whiskey too?'

'I'm sure,' Falkner answered in measured tones.

Skye gave him a searching look. He looked calm enough, his gaze steadily meeting hers, and yet there was a certain wariness in that gaze too, leading her to the conclusion that there was still something Falkner wasn't telling her…

'Falkner, you said just now that the lawyer wants to see "us",' she realized huskily.

He grimaced. 'So I did.'

'Well?' she prompted as he added nothing further.

'Skye, how old are you?'

'How—? What on earth does that have to do with anything?' she demanded exasperatedly.

'Quite a lot, actually.' He grimaced.

There definitely was something else he hadn't told her yet, something that he knew, from the grim expression on his face, that she wasn't going to like.

'You may as well tell me, Falkner,' she sighed.

'Your birthday is in February, isn't it?'

She frowned. 'How did you know that?'

He shrugged. 'Your father must have mentioned it. February, right?'

'Right,' she confirmed warily.

'That's what I thought.' Falkner nodded slowly. 'Skye, the money your father made through his investments with me he put into a trust for you in his will until you reach the age of twenty-five.'

She blinked. 'He did?'

Falkner gave the ghost of a smile. 'He did. In seven months time you are going to inherit that money.' He named a sum of money that, after the last six months of hardship for both Skye and her father, left Skye speechless.

Her father had done all that, made all that money, and put it in trust for her, without so much as telling her a thing about it? It seemed incredible!

It also seemed something else...

'He knew, didn't he?' Skye said slowly. 'That O'Hara Whiskey, no matter how he tried to save it, would one day go down,' she explained at Falkner's questioning look. 'He knew, and he made provision for me.'

'With hindsight, I can say yes, I think that's exactly what he did.' Falkner nodded abruptly. 'At the time he made the will, I had no idea, of course. But knowing what I do now about your uncle Seamus's involvement in the downfall of O'Hara Whiskey, I'm sure that

Connor set up a trust for you, made from money completely separate from the company, so that your life wouldn't be ruined by it too.'

Skye felt the sting of tears in her eyes. Her father, despite his death, was still taking care of her. But she would have given up all of it, the money, that financial security, just to have him back!

'Skye!' Falkner groaned as the tears fell gently down her cheeks, reaching across the table to tightly grasp one of her hands in his. 'It will be all right, Skye!' he assured her fiercely.

No, it wouldn't, it wouldn't ever be all right again. No matter what provision her father had made for her, it wouldn't bring him back. And crying all over Falkner wasn't going to make it any easier, either!

She moved her hand from his grasp to brush the tears impatiently from her cheeks, stiffening her spine determinedly before meeting his gaze across the table. 'What's the catch, Falkner?' she prompted frowningly.

He raised dark brows. 'Catch?'

Her mouth twisted into a humourless smile. 'What is your involvement in this?' she prompted dryly. 'Apart from the fact that my father entrusted you with the information about the trust in the first place,' she added haltingly.

She still found that amazing. But, then, she had been constantly surprised these last few weeks at the depth of her father's friendship with this man...

Falkner drew in a sharp breath. 'As I told you, the money has been put in trust until you reach the age of twenty-five.'

Which was only seven months away; she already had a job, was perfectly capable of supporting herself for as long as she had to. Besides, now that she knew about the money, she intended using some of it to help her uncle Seamus.

'Skye, the trust has two trustees,' Falkner bit out forcefully as she continued to look at him wordlessly. 'For obvious legal reasons, your father's lawyer is one of those trustees—'

'And you're the other one!' she suddenly realized, staring incredulously across the table at Falkner.

She was right, she knew she was right, could see by the sudden bleakness of Falkner's expression as he steadily met her accusing gaze that was exactly what he was trying—not very successfully so far!—to tell her.

Falkner was her trustee, almost the equivalent of a guardian, was her financial guardian! Well…one of them. Falkner—of all people her father could have chosen!

But why had her father chosen Falkner, a man Skye hadn't even seen for six years, let alone anything else?

Because her father had trusted him…

One thing she did know, had always known, was that her father's love for her was absolute, that her happiness was his main concern in life. And he would never have entrusted her happiness to a man he didn't also trust absolutely.

And yet he had never told her of the trust fund he had set up for her in his will, let alone that he had made Falkner Harrington one of its trustees…

Perhaps because her father had hoped it would never be necessary for her to need to know? After all, her father had still been a young man, had been fighting to the end to maintain some sort of business reputation, could have had no idea that he would die so suddenly shortly before her twenty-fifth birthday. He also knew

Skye well enough to know she would hate even the thought that he had made such a provision for her, and the implications behind it.

Although that didn't explain why Falkner hadn't told her about this earlier…

'You are, aren't you?' she prompted accusingly.

He gave a heavy sigh. 'I am.' He nodded.

'Great! Just great!' Skye muttered frustratedly.

'Just when you thought it was safe to go back in the water,' Falkner muttered.

She frowned. 'I beg your pardon?'

'Never mind.' He gave a dismissive shake of his head. 'I realize you aren't exactly thrilled at the prospect of this trusteeship, Skye, but—'

'You can't possibly know how unthrilled I am, Falkner,' she cut in forcefully.

The idea of never seeing Falkner again was a painful one for her, but the idea of being tied to him by his financial control—of his being tied to her for the same reason!—was also unacceptable to her.

His mouth twisted humourlessly. 'I think I can hazard a guess,' he murmured self-derisively. 'Look, Skye, I didn't have to tell you any of this tonight, could have just—'

'Oh, yes, you did,' she scorned. 'Because you knew exactly how I would have reacted if I just heard it cold from the lawyer,' she added accusingly as he would have spoken.

He gave a heavy sigh. 'Why not look on the bright side, Skye? It's only for another seven months—and then you can tell me all over again exactly what I can do with my friendship!'

She didn't want to tell him what he could do with his friendship—it was the fact that he only had friendship to offer that made it all so unbearable. If he felt only a little of the deep love for her that she had for him, then it would all be so different!

'I can't wait,' she assured him with feeling. 'I don't think I can eat any of this.' She pushed her plate away uninterestedly.

Falkner's expression darkened. 'Not eating isn't going to solve anything!'

She glared across at him. 'Would you rather I was ill in the restaurant?'

'I would rather you ate your meal,' he came back hardly.

'Like a good little girl!' Skye shot back at him sharply.

Falkner grimaced, shaking his head. 'I somehow doubt you were ever that. In fact, I distinctly remember you as being extremely precocious at almost eighteen!'

Skye felt the colour warm her cheeks at this reminder of what had happened between them six years ago. 'I was hardly a "little girl" at eighteen!' she snapped back.

'No?' He raised mocking brows.

'No!' she bit out challengingly. 'So when am I supposed to go and see this lawyer?' She changed the subject abruptly, having no intention of eating any more of the pâté.

'When are we supposed to go and see the lawyer,' Falkner corrected lightly.

'I don't see why you need to be there.' Skye shook her head. 'After all, you already know what's in my fathers will,' she added accusingly.

He gave an abrupt inclination of his head. 'Which is precisely why I have to be there.'

'I can't believe this,' Skye muttered frustratedly. 'What on earth was my father thinking of?' she groaned.

'You,' Falkner answered unhesitantly.

Skye's anger deflated like the air out of a balloon, her shoulders slumping as she sat back weakly in her chair.

Whatever she might think about this situation, however intolerable it was to her to have Falkner as her financial trustee for the next seven months, she knew that her father would only ever have acted in a way he felt was best for her. The fact that she didn't feel the same way about his choice wasn't her father's fault.

She had never confided in her father how she felt about Falkner, and it was because she hadn't confided in him that her father couldn't possibly have realized how much she would hate being dependent on Falkner in this way.

'Yes,' she accepted with a shaky sigh. 'When would you like to go and see the lawyer?'

'I suggested tomorrow afternoon, at four o'clock, might be a good time?' Falkner looked at her questioningly.

The word 'suggest' and Falkner didn't quite go together, but she understood exactly what he meant! 'In other words, you've made an appointment for us to see the lawyer at four o'clock tomorrow afternoon?' she said dryly.

He nodded. 'Subject to your approval, of course.'

'Oh, of course,' Skye derided, at the same time mulling the idea over in her mind.

If her work schedule tomorrow went anything like today, then she should have a couple of hours free in the afternoon before the second feeding time in the evening. She certainly wasn't going to ask for time off on only her second day at work!

'Yes, I think four o'clock tomorrow will be okay,' she said slowly. 'If it isn't I'll let you know.'

'Skye, I need to know—'

'You don't have the right to ask, Falkner,' she warned softly, easily guessing that he was again going to ask where she was now staying.

His mouth tightened grimly. 'I disagree—'

'Then we'll just have to disagree, won't we?' Skye cut in determinedly. 'You may be one of my financial trustees, Falkner, but that doesn't give you any rights over the rest of my life.'

He drew in a sharp breath. 'You aren't making this easy for me, Skye.'

She gave a humourless laugh. 'I don't think this is going to be easy for either of us, Falkner.' She shook her head. 'But no doubt we'll cope.'

'No doubt we'll have to,' he acknowledged bleakly. 'You know, I don't think Connor ever intended for it to be this way,' he added gently.

'Probably not,' she conceded heavily, knowing that her father could have no idea how much she would hate this dependency on Falkner, of all people.

Falkner reached out and lightly clasped her hand as it rested on the table-top. 'Can't we try to be friends, Skye?' he prompted huskily.

How could the two of them ever be friends, when it was so much more than that she wanted from him?

She moved her hand from his grasp. 'We weren't friends before, Falkner, so why should we become so now?' she dismissed hardly.

'For your father's sake?' he prompted huskily.

She swallowed hard, her eyes pained as she looked across the table at him. 'That was unfair, Falkner.' She shook her head.

'Maybe,' he conceded heavily. 'But think about it, hmm?'

Skye had plenty of time to think during the sleepless night that followed the evening out with Falkner.

Part of her was elated at the thought of not being completely cut off from seeing Falkner, but another part of her was distraught at the reason behind it.

There was something else troubling her too, something about the last few days that bothered her and yet eluded her at the same time, something that Falkner had said or done that didn't seem to quite add up. But with all the other thoughts that bombarded her, she just couldn't think what it was…

CHAPTER ELEVEN

'I KNEW you were reckless, but I didn't realize you were insane, too!'

Skye had dropped the bucket of water she was carrying at the first sound of Falkner's voice directly behind her, turning to look at him accusingly even as the water soaked into her jeans and trainers. 'Do you have to keep creeping up on me in this way?' she snapped impatiently, two bright spots of angry colour in her cheek as she glared at him. 'The name Houdini springs to mind!'

Falkner returned that gaze unrepentantly, his own impatience obvious from his grim expression. 'What the hell do you think you're doing?' he rasped, moving further into the stable where Skye was working.

Skye eyed him scathingly. 'What does it look like I'm doing?' She bent to pick up the now-empty bucket. 'I'll have to fill this up again now,' she muttered irritably, all the time aware that her irritation was partly due to her complete awareness of Falkner; just being close to him like this made her tremble.

Falkner reached out a slender hand and easily took the bucket from her grasp. 'I don't think so,' he told her harshly.

Her brows rose at his autocratic tone. 'Oh, you don't?' she echoed in a dangerously soft voice.

Quite what Falkner was doing here at the stables where she was working, she had no idea—although she could take a pretty good guess! Somehow Falkner had learnt where she was staying, after all—probably from that grapevine he had mentioned!—and he obviously wasn't pleased at the knowledge. In fact, he hadn't even been able to wait another four hours, until they were due to meet anyway, in order to tell her how displeased he was!

'No, I don't,' Falkner bit out tersely. 'Are you completely insane, or only mildly so?' He arched blond brows over icy blue eyes.

She deliberately gave the question some thought. 'Only mildly so, I think,' she finally answered him. 'But I can't be sure,' she added challengingly. Challenging him was better than throwing herself into his arms! she decided.

'I can,' he rasped grimly, putting the bucket firmly to one side before turning back to her. 'Have you forgotten that you broke your ribs only two weeks ago?'

Of course she hadn't forgotten. It was impossible for her to do that. When she'd woken up this morning her body had seemed to ache everywhere, not just her ribs, and it had taken her almost half an hour to get out of bed, wash, and get dressed. The aches in the rest of her body had eased as she'd joined in the busy morning routine of the stable, but the ache in her ribs seemed, if anything, to be worse.

'What does that have to do with anything?' she snapped.

'Everything!' Falkner exploded. 'For goodness' sake, Skye, I told you last night that you don't have to work—'

'You told me no such thing,' she returned just as angrily, her hands clenched into fists at her sides. 'If you're referring to the trust fund, I'm not twenty-five for another seven months, remember?'

'But as the trustees of your trust fund, Peter Bryant and myself are empowered to use our discretion as to the distribution of those funds until such time as you are twenty-five!' Falkner glared down at her.

'Well, no one told me that!' Skye snapped forcefully.

If it weren't for the disparity in their heights, she and Falkner would have been nose to nose at that moment, both of them furious, chins jutting, eyes glaring.

Falkner seemed to see the funny side of the situation only seconds after Skye, his mouth twitching as he tried to hold back a smile, some of the tension leaving his body as he sighed. 'No, they didn't, did they?' he conceded wryly. 'Well, we do. And we will. We'll discuss and agree on that when we meet at four o'clock this afternoon. In the meantime, why don't you get your things—?'

'I beg your pardon?' She frowned.

'Get your things,' Falkner repeated evenly. 'I've already spoken to James, and he's quite happy for you to leave immediately—'

'You've spoken to James Hurley?' Skye said slowly. Even she hadn't spoken to the owner of the stables, all of her dealings so far having been through the stable manager.

Falkner gave a humourless smile. 'I told you this is a small community, Skye; James and I have known each other for years.'

Why was that no surprise? But even so—!

'Well, I'm sure that's very nice for you both.' She didn't even try to disguise her sarcasm. 'But what does that have to do with my working here?' She raised challenging brows.

Falkner's eyes narrowed ominously. 'I've explained the situation to James—'

'What "situation"?' Skye cut in sharply. So far no one working at the stable seemed to have recognized her as the daughter of Connor O'Hara who had been so much in the newspapers recently, or, if they had, they hadn't been interested enough to pursue the subject...

'The fact that you were recently involved in a car accident "situation", of course,' Falkner enlarged impatiently. 'I'm not completely insensitive, Skye—'

'No?' She was too angry at the moment to care how insulting she was being; angry at Falkner for searching her out here, angry with herself because she felt at any moment as if she might cry again, most of all angry because she knew she wanted nothing more than to launch herself into his arms, to kiss him, and be kissed back by him, until they were both senseless!

She might also be outwardly furious at Falkner for what appeared to be his high-handedness in telling James Hurley she would no longer be working here, but what made it all the more unbearable was that inwardly she had already come to the same conclusion; she really wasn't physically up to doing this sort of work yet, the ache in her ribs only slightly dulled by taking a couple of the pain-killers given to her when she'd left the hospital.

Falkner had drawn in a sharp breath at her deliberate insult, his face pale now, a nerve pulsing in his tightly clenched jaw. 'No,' he confirmed, his voice sounding as if it came over broken glass. 'Skye, are you deliberately trying to kill yourself?' he rasped harshly.

Now it was Skye's turn to pale, her eyes suddenly huge in that paleness. 'No, of course not—'

'What do you think is going to happen if one of those broken ribs moves and pierces one of your lungs?' he cut in softly. 'What if you're alone in one of the stables here when it happens? What if—'

'Okay, okay, I get the picture!' she assured him exasperatedly—because once again she knew he was right.

'Good.' He nodded abruptly. 'Now, are you going to get your things or do you want me to get them?'

'I think you've already had enough dealings with my things, thank you very much!' She still felt embarrassed at the thought of his having been to the hotel in London and packed her belongings for her—especially the silky underwear! 'I'll get my own things,' she assured him firmly. 'Then, if it's not too much trouble, I would like you to drive me back to the hotel,' she added determinedly.

'No,' he answered unhesitantly.

Skye turned sharply on her way out of the stable. 'What do you mean no?' she gasped.

'Exactly what I said,' he returned calmly. 'As I see it, you have two choices: you can either come and stay with me, or—'

'I am not staying with you!' she burst out frustratedly.

'Why not?' he taunted.

'Because—because I'm not!' she finally managed impatiently. The way she felt about him, this complete awareness she had of him, she simply couldn't bear to be with him in such close proximity.

'I'm sorry you feel that way.' He grimaced. 'Maybe you will find the second choice more acceptable? Belinda and Charles would love to have you stay with them until you find somewhere of your own,' he explained at Skye's questioning look.

Once again she felt that prick of tears at the kindness she had encountered from the Harrington family; for all that she fought against what she considered Falkner's arrogant high-handedness, she was also aware that he was acting out of kindness, if not personally to her, then out of his affection for her father. Belinda and Charles had also gone out of their way to be kind.

'And it goes without saying that the twins are wholeheartedly for the idea of having you stay with them,' Falkner added ruefully at her continued silence.

She gave a shaky smile at the thought of the adorable duo; Lissa and Jemmy's innocence, their utter delight with life, might be just what she needed right now.

'Do I take it that's a yes to the second choice?' Falkner drawled dryly.

'Yes,' Skye confirmed huskily.

'Good,' he accepted briskly. 'Now can we get out of here?' he prompted tightly.

Skye gave him a searching look. She had thought he'd looked grim and tense when he'd arrived because of the expected opposition from her to his suggestion, but perhaps there was a second reason for his strained look…?

Until three years ago this, the stables, the noise and bustle, the unmistakable smell of horses, had been his world. Oh, he still kept a small stable at his estate, but nothing like this…

'Yes, of course,' she agreed briskly.

Falkner didn't even try to hide his surprise at her sudden acquiescence. 'Did I miss something?' He frowned.

Skye gave him a mocking glance. 'Not that I'm aware of,' she dismissed. 'Believe it or not, Falkner,

I'm not completely unreasonable.' She deliberately used a similar phrase to his earlier one.

'I'll have to take your word for that,' he murmured dryly as he closed the stable door behind them. 'I've seen little evidence of it so far,' he added at her questioning look.

She shrugged. 'Maybe you haven't been looking hard enough.'

He chuckled softly. 'Are you ever at a loss for words?'

'I told you before—rarely,' she instantly came back.

Falkner gave a rueful shake of his head. 'I'll wait in the Range Rover for you while you get your things. Oh, I almost forgot to give you this.' He took an envelope from his denims pocket. 'It's only your wages, Skye,' he explained at her wary expression. 'James gave them to me earlier to pass on to you.'

'Thanks.' She took the envelope. Her first ever wage packet—even if it was only for one day!

Falkner nodded. 'Apparently you were very good at your job; James said if you ever want to come back to give him a call,' he told her dryly.

Skye felt a warm glow at the praise. She might have been in extreme discomfort the last couple of days, but she had enjoyed working with the horses; it was nice to know her efforts had been appreciated.

'Which, of course, you aren't going to do,' Falkner added firmly.

Her eyes widened in surprise. 'I'm not?'

He sighed. 'Skye, with the money you will receive in seven months' time, you could open your own stable!'

'Ah.' She nodded slowly, busying herself by putting her wage envelope in her pocket.

Avoiding Falkner's probing gaze was what she was

really doing, she inwardly acknowledged ruefully. He was altogether too astute, too knowing, for her to actually let him see the emotions in her own expressive eyes.

'Skye…?'

Her expression was deliberately innocent as she looked up at him enquiringly.

He frowned. 'What are you up to…?'

'Up to…?' she repeated in a puzzled voice. 'What on earth makes you think I'm up to something, Falkner?'

Too far, too innocent, Skye, she instantly admonished herself as she saw Falkner's eyes narrow speculatively at her dismissive reply.

'I have a younger sister, remember,' he said slowly, his gaze still wary.

'And very nice she is, too,' Skye answered briskly. 'It really is very kind of Belinda and Charles to offer to let me stay with them in this way.'

'They all like you very much,' Falkner answered distractedly.

'I like them too.' She nodded, very much aware that his distraction wasn't in the right direction; namely, away from what she was 'up to'! 'Shouldn't we be on our way now if I'm to get settled in, showered and changed, before our appointment with the lawyer this afternoon?' she prompted lightly as he still hung back.

'Skye…?'

She gave him another quizzical look. 'Yes?'

His eyes were narrowed. 'What aren't you telling me?'

She shook her head, deliberately meeting his searching gaze. 'I have no idea what you're talking about.'

'There is something… Have you seen any more of Paul Barclay?' he prompted abruptly.

'Paul—? Oh, you mean the vet I met at the barbecue

on Sunday,' she realized dazedly. 'No, of course I haven't,' she dismissed frowningly.

'Do you intend seeing him again?' Falkner persisted grimly.

'Not that I'm aware.' She shrugged, in total confusion as to what had prompted this line of questioning.

Paul Barclay had seemed quite a pleasant man, charming and friendly as well as quite good-looking. But Skye certainly had no intention of becoming involved with him. Or, indeed, anyone else. She wouldn't be staying in the area long enough for that!

She gave Falkner a quizzical look. 'He was a friend of your wife's, wasn't he?' she probed softly.

Falkner's mouth tightened. 'One of many,' he confirmed harshly. 'And none of them meant a damn thing to her. Selina liked to have more than one admirer at a time,' he explained scathingly. 'Barclay came way down her list of male interests, I'm afraid,' he added grimly.

And yet Falkner's wife had been the one to divorce him amid claims of 'another woman'…

'Well, I have no intention of seeing him again,' Skye told Falkner sharply. 'I'll go and get my things and meet you at the Range Rover.' She turned abruptly and walked off in the direction of the staff accommodation.

Could Falkner possibly still be in love with Selina? He had been pretty definite the other day when he had assured Belinda he would never marry again. Could that be because he was still in love with his ex-wife?

One thing Skye now knew for certain: the sooner she got away from here—from Falkner—the better!

CHAPTER TWELVE

'NO!'

FALKNER said nothing else, no explanation, just that emphatic no!

How dared he? Skye fumed inwardly. Just who did Falkner think he was?

Two bright spots of angry colour burned in her cheeks as she turned to glare at him. 'I was talking to Mr Bryant, actually,' she bit out furiously.

Falkner shook his head. 'I don't care who you were talking to—the answer is still no,' he bit out succinctly.

The two of them were seated in Peter Bryant's office, facing the lawyer as he sat behind his desk. And the poor man looked totally bewildered by the antagonism that suddenly seemed to have erupted in his otherwise quiet offices.

Peter Bryant was her father's English lawyer, the senior partner of Bryant, Bryant and Ogilvie, Skye had discovered when they had arrived ten minutes ago, a tall, thin man in his late fifties, his hair iron-grey, his eyes a kindly brown.

Although those eyes looked totally perplexed at the moment!

Was that any wonder? The preliminary politeness over, Skye had just got through telling the lawyer that she needed an advance on her trust fund so that she could return to Ireland—only to have Falkner cut in on the conversation in that implacable way.

'Surely it's reasonable for Miss O'Hara to want to return to Ireland?' the lawyer prompted now. 'If only to settle her affairs,' he added with a sympathetic smile in her direction.

'If that were the reason Skye were going back, it would be perfectly reasonable,' Falkner allowed grimly, dressed formally this afternoon in a dark suit and snowy white shirt, his grey tie knotted precisely at his throat. 'But that isn't the reason—is it?' he prompted, blue eyes hard as he refused to let her drop her gaze from his.

Too astute. Too knowing.

She drew in a sharp breath. 'I—'

'The truth, Skye,' Falkner warned softly. 'Peter may not know you as well as I do, but I can assure you he isn't going to be best pleased when he finds out you've deceived him about why you want this money.'

'He's my uncle, Falkner!' she defended fiercely.

Originally she had intended doing all she could to help her uncle Seamus when the money came to her in seven months' time, at the same time realizing it might be too late by then, and Falkner's suggestion that she could have an advance on the trust fund had seemed heaven-sent...

Except that Falkner had obviously realized exactly why she wanted the money!

'He's my uncle, Falkner,' she repeated huskily, her hands clasped tightly together. 'I could use that money to help him—'

'And do you think that's what your father intended it to be used for?' he cut in softly.

Probably not, if, as Falkner had claimed, he had set up the trust fund for her after he had known of her uncle's embezzlement. But, at the same time, her father couldn't have just expected her to sit back and let her uncle go to prison without at least trying to help him, either!

She straightened, her chin raised determinedly. 'My father would have expected me to do what was right,' she said firmly.

Falkner's expression softened slightly as he looked at her. 'Yes, he would,' he acknowledged gently. 'Just as he expected me to do what was right, too—'

'My father would never condone your allowing his brother to go to prison without at least putting up some sort of fight!' Skye turned on him heatedly.

Falkner met her gaze unflinchingly for several seconds before turning to the other man. 'Peter, would you read out the last provision of Connor's will?'

'Certainly.' Peter Bryant hastened to agree as he put on a pair of half-glasses.

The poor man looked pleased to have something official to do in the face of all the emotion he had been subjected to the last few minutes, Skye noted ruefully.

'"Lastly, I give to my good friend, Falkner Harrington, all my shares in his possession in order that he might sell them and use the sale proceeds to aid my brother, Seamus O'Hara, should the need arise",' he read evenly, before looking at Skye over the top of his glasses. 'That would be the uncle you were referring to?'

'Yes,' she confirmed huskily, unable to even look at Falkner now.

She should have known her father wouldn't have just

abandoned her uncle Seamus, should have realized that he would make some sort of provision for his older brother.

'It's already taken care of, Skye,' Falkner told her quietly. 'A lawyer has already been hired to represent your uncle. Your father had already paid back as much of the money as he could, and the sale of the estate and other assets should take care of the rest of it. Taking all that into account, plus the fact that your uncle sought out the police himself and confessed, the lawyer seems to think that your uncle may get away with a light sentence.'

Skye's relief at hearing all this was immense. But at the same time she couldn't help wondering why Falkner hadn't told her all of this earlier...

'In the circumstances, will you still be requiring the same amount of money, Miss O'Hara?' Peter Bryant prompted formally.

'Yes—'

'No—'

Skye looked frowningly at Falkner as they both answered at the same time, she in the affirmative, Falkner in the negative.

'Whether here—or in Ireland,' she added wryly, 'I'm going to need money to buy a house, and to keep myself, until I decide what—what I'm going to do with the rest of my life,' she concluded flatly; because any life she made for herself wouldn't include Falkner!

Falkner's mouth tightened. 'And I think it's far too early for you to be making any of those decisions,' he rasped.

'It wasn't too early for you to ask me to marry you!' she returned hotly.

There it was again, that 'something' that kept niggling in the back of her mind, that 'something' that didn't add up, that 'something' she couldn't quite get straight in her mind, that 'something' that didn't quite make sense…

None of this made sense! Not one single thing had since the moment her father had died!

'Never mind. Forget I said that,' she dismissed impatiently, bending to pick up her bag before standing up. 'I'll have to come back and see you some other time, Mr Bryant,' she told him heavily, grimacing slightly as she saw his shocked expression. 'I'm afraid I can't think straight just now—'

'Exactly,' Falkner concurred grimly, also standing up.

She turned to him with pained eyes. 'You're most of the reason I can't think straight,' she told him shakily. 'You say one thing, and do another, and I—' She stopped abruptly as her voice broke emotionally. 'I have to get out of here!' She turned and made a bolt for the door.

As she had known he would, Falkner caught up with her once she was outside on the pavement, but that didn't stop her flinching as his arm moved protectively about her waist as he guided her to the Range Rover.

She turned and buried her head against his shoulder, the tears falling hotly down her cheeks.

'This doesn't get any easier, does it?' he murmured gently, stopping beside the Range Rover to gather her fully into his arms.

Skye shook her head wordlessly, wishing she could just stay here for ever, safe in Falkner's arms.

'You know, it might be a little less—painful, if you stopped fighting me.' Falkner spoke softly into the hair at her temple. 'Don't you know yet that I would never do anything that would harm you?'

'I do know,' she assured him huskily. 'I just—' She shook her head. 'I don't understand—'

'It's too soon, Skye,' he comforted gently. 'And from what you just said in Peter Bryant's office, I didn't help to make it any less confusing by asking you to marry me,' he murmured self-derisively. 'Forget I ever mentioned the subject, hmm?'

That didn't help to make her feel in the least better—because if Falkner had repeated the marriage proposal right now, she knew she would have accepted, and just hoped that one day he might come to love her!

'Of course.' She pulled out of his arms, her gaze not quite able to meet his. 'Could we just go back to Belinda's now? I think I need a little time to myself.'

'I don't think you stand too much chance of that with the Terrible Twins around!' Falkner teased as he unlocked the car doors, seeing her safely settled inside before going round to get in behind the wheel.

It wasn't time away from the twins she needed, or even Belinda and Charles; it was Falkner that always threw her into such confusion…

Belinda and Charles couldn't have been more welcoming when Skye and Falkner arrived at their home a short time later, Belinda taking her up the stairs to the room she would be using during her stay so that she could change.

'This is lovely,' Skye told the other woman gratefully as she looked around the gold and cream room, even a vase of flowers on the dressing table to welcome her. 'It really is kind of you and Charles to—'

'Don't, Skye.' Belinda reached out and squeezed her arm reassuringly. 'We're only too pleased to have you here.'

'Thank you, anyway,' Skye told her huskily.

The two men were seated comfortably in the sitting room sharing a glass of whisky when Skye and Belinda rejoined them a few minutes later.

Although Falkner stood up as soon as the two women entered the room. 'Everything okay?' he prompted Skye huskily.

'Fine.' She nodded, not quite able to meet his gaze.

'Good.' He smiled. 'I'll just pop through to the kitchen and see the twins before I leave,' he told Belinda before putting down his empty whisky glass.

His sister frowned across at him. 'But I thought you would be staying for dinner…?'

Falkner gave a rueful grimace. 'It's a nice thought, Belinda, but I think Skye has seen quite enough of me for one day!'

If the circumstances had been different, Skye knew she would never want him to leave. As it was, she didn't want to be the one responsible for driving him away from his own sister's house! 'Do stay, Falkner,' she encouraged huskily.

He gave her a probing look, his own expression guarded, finally giving a slight shake of his head. 'I won't, if you don't mind. I have some calls to make, anyway,' he added briskly as Belinda would have protested.

Of course, she had once again taken him away from his own business interests with the necessity he had at the moment to be involved with hers, Skye realized guiltily.

Charles stood up. 'I'll walk outside with you,' he said lightly.

Falkner moved to give his sister a kiss on the cheek before glancing across at the pale-faced Skye. 'I'll give you a call some time tomorrow,' he told her huskily.

She didn't know what to say. Part of her so wanted him to stay, but another part of her knew that, for the moment, they had nothing more to say to each other...

'I'm really sorry about that, Skye,' Belinda apologized frowningly once the two men had left the room. 'I'm really not sure what's happened to Falkner's manners just recently!' she added disgustedly.

'It isn't Falkner's fault,' Skye instantly defended him. 'I—it's mine,' she added miserably.

'Don't be silly,' Belinda dismissed briskly.

'But it is,' Skye insisted. 'Falkner doesn't need all this in his life.'

'Skye, your father was his friend,' the older woman told her gently.

She was only just beginning to appreciate what good friends the two men must have been, what a loss it was to Falkner, too...

'Yes.' She nodded. 'But this present situation is difficult, to say the least.' She grimaced. 'And I'm afraid I didn't help matters this afternoon by blurting out, in front of the lawyer, that Falkner had asked me to marry him!'

She had just done it again, Skye realized with an inward groan as Belinda blinked dazedly at this disclosure!

CHAPTER THIRTEEN

'Skye—'

'I shouldn't have told you that!' Skye put in hurriedly, wincing slightly as she saw the open speculation in Belinda's eyes. 'I don't suppose I could ask you to forget I ever said it?' she prompted awkwardly.

'No, you certainly couldn't,' Belinda assured her laughingly, obviously having recovered slightly from her shock. 'Falkner really asked you to marry him?' she prompted slowly.

'Yes. But only because he feels sorry for me,' Skye hastened to explain, really wishing she hadn't said anything; she could tell by the other woman's determined expression that there was no way Belinda was going to let the subject go!

'Rubbish!' Belinda answered unhesitantly.

Skye blinked at her certainty. 'But he does—'

'Rubbish,' the other woman repeated dismissively. 'He may feel sorry for the situation, but, I can assure you, that certainly isn't enough to nudge him into making a marriage proposal! I suppose it's too much to hope that you said yes...?' She raised dark brows.

'Of course I didn't say yes!' Skye told her incredulously; Belinda couldn't really think it was a good idea that Skye and Falkner marry each other—could she? 'Falkner doesn't really want to marry me.' She shook her head. 'I told you, he just feels sorry for me.'

'And I believe I said that was rubbish,' Belinda said dryly.

'Twice!'

'Yes, you did.' She gave a rueful smile. 'But I have no idea why you should think that?' It was her turn to look at Belinda frowningly now.

'Several things, actually,' the other woman told her lightly. 'Tell me, Skye, when did you and Falkner actually meet?'

She frowned. 'I thought you knew, he came to the hospital a week after the accident—'

'No, not this time,' Belinda cut in. 'When did the two of you first meet at all?'

'Six years ago,' Skye answered unhesitantly. Six years, six months, and five days ago, to be precise. She could probably even give the hours if she thought about it for a minute or two!

'I thought as much.' Belinda looked triumphant before giving a glance at her wrist-watch. 'I'm afraid it's time now to do homework with the twins, before we bath them and get them up to bed,' she explained regretfully. 'But we will get back to this, Skye,' she assured her determinedly. 'I love Falkner dearly, you know, but he can be such an idiot at times!'

Skye couldn't help it, she laughed; it was so strange to hear anyone talk in this derogatory way about the assured Falkner Harrington that she knew. And loved. Although, as his sister, probably no one had more right to do so than Belinda!

'While you're waiting, perhaps you would like to take a look through this,' the other woman suggested, rummaging in the depths of a cupboard beneath the dresser to pull out what looked like a photograph album. 'Don't worry, I'm not a doting mother about to bore you with dozens of photographs of her offspring.' Belinda laughed at Skye's dazed expression as she gave her the album. 'There are just several photographs in here that I think you might find interesting,' she added with a pointed rise of her brows. 'In the meantime, make yourself at home. Take that through to the kitchen with you and make yourself a cup of coffee; Charles and I will be down in an hour or so. The important thing to remember is that Falkner met you first,' she added enigmatically before hurrying from the room in search of the rest of her family.

Skye made her way slowly to the kitchen, finding its rusticity entirely to her liking as she moved about the room making the suggested coffee, putting off the moment when she would sit down at the old oak table that stood at one end of the room and open the photograph album Belinda had given her. There were sure to be several photographs of Falkner in there, and, much as she loved him, a photograph just wouldn't do when it was the real flesh and blood man she so ached for!

The first few pages of photographs were innocuous enough; several photographs of Belinda's 'offspring', looking as adorable as babies as they did now as they beamed up at the camera with gummy smiles.

The next few pages of photographs were of couples or families formally grouped, and Skye had reached almost halfway through the album before the first photograph of Falkner appeared, looking extremely formal in a morning suit, Charles standing at his side looking just as handsome in a similar suit, both men having carnations pinned in their button-holes.

She was looking at a wedding album!

Not just any wedding album, but Falkner's wedding album!

Undoubtedly the photographs had been taken from Belinda's point of view rather than any other, concentrated on the children, the Harrington family, and of course Charles and Falkner, but nevertheless Skye was absolutely positive that these were the photographs taken at Falkner's wedding to Selina.

Her hands trembled as she pushed the album sharply away from her across the table, staring at the album now as if it were a snake about to bite her.

Why on earth had Belinda given her such a thing? She had thought the other woman liked her. But surely Belinda must know—

Know what? That Skye would be upset at seeing the photographs of Falkner's wedding to Selina?

And why should she assume that Belinda would know that? After all, for years she had gone out of her way to conceal her feelings for Falkner from other people, including her beloved father.

But even so it seemed a very strange thing for Belinda to do…

Skye swallowed hard, the first shock having receded, curiosity starting to take its place. As Belinda had known that it would? She was quickly learning that it didn't do to underestimate the seemingly uncomplicated Belinda…

She reached out to slowly pull the album back in front of her, turning over the page, only to find herself confronted with the first picture of the bride and groom together as they walked down the aisle after the ceremony.

After that, Skye was hooked, turning each successive page over more quickly than the last, the truth of Belinda's intent finally dawning on her. No wonder Belinda and Paul Barclay had initially mistaken her for Selina—facially the two of them might have been sisters, if not exactly twins.

Selina was taller than Skye, reached up to Falkner's chin, whereas Skye only managed his shoulders; Selina was also much older than Skye, probably in her late twenties when these photographs were taken, and the other woman was also in possession of those voluptuous curves Skye had so coveted when she was younger, but the two faces, the sky-blue eyes, the creamy complexion, even the blazing copper-bronze hair, were almost identical!

What did it mean? More to the point, what did Belinda think that it meant? Because Skye was becoming more and more convinced that Belinda thought it meant something!

Skye sat back heavily in her chair, still staring at the photographs of a grim-faced Falkner and the beautiful Selina taken at their wedding reception.

A year after their own disastrous first meeting, Falkner had married a woman who facially could have been her double. Facially, because from the little Skye had gleaned from other people concerning the other woman's nature, the two bore little resemblance there; if Skye had been the one lucky enough to be Falkner's wife she would never even have looked at another man, let alone become involved with any of them!

She turned sharply as she heard someone enter the

kitchen behind her, Belinda standing just inside the doorway, her head tilted sideways in silent query.

Skye swallowed hard, still confused by Selina's likeness to her, even more confused as to why Belinda thought she should see that. But also knowing she had to find out the answer to those questions. And, in fairness, there was really only one person who could give her those answers...

She licked dry lips, having totally forgotten to drink the coffee she had made for herself earlier. 'I know he said he had some calls to make, but do you think Falkner will be at home this evening?' Her voice was husky too.

'I'm sure he will,' Belinda confirmed softly. 'After all, what reason does he have to go out?' she added ruefully.

Skye stood up with a noisy scrape of the chair on the tiled floor.

'Take the station wagon,' Belinda invited even as she took the keys down from the rack behind the kitchen door. 'Will you be okay driving yourself?' she added as the thought suddenly occurred to her.

'Fine,' Skye assured her as she took the keys. 'I could be about to make a colossal fool of myself, you know, Belinda,' she added, the nervousness increasing inside her by the minute at what she was about to do.

The other woman gave a confident shake of her head. 'I don't think so.'

Skye could only hope Belinda was right. Could only hope that she was right in the conclusions she had come to only seconds ago. Because if she was wrong—!

'Here, take this with you.' Belinda reached to take a bag off one of the work surfaces. 'It's some wool Mrs Graham asked me to get so that she can knit the twins a jumper each for the winter,' she explained ruefully.

'Feeble, I know, but it's better than nothing,' she added with a grimace.

Skye took the bag before moving to give the other woman a hug. 'You're a sister in a million, Belinda.'

'Tell Falkner that!' The other woman chuckled softly as she stepped back.

'Oh, I think he already knows,' Skye said with certainty.

'Good luck,' Belinda told her huskily.

Skye had a feeling she was going to need it!

Handing over the wool to Mrs Graham was no problem, although, not surprisingly, the housekeeper did look slightly surprised that Skye had driven over purposefully to give it to her.

Skye had deliberately gone to the back door of the house in order to deliver the wool, not wanting to alert Falkner to her presence just yet.

'Is that for Falkner?' Skye looked at the tray the other woman had been preparing when she'd arrived.

The housekeeper instantly looked disapproving. 'He says he isn't hungry.' She shook her head. 'He's been completely off his food just lately, but I thought he might eat some home-made soup and bread if I put it in front of him.'

Skye wondered just how recent that 'lately' was that Falkner had been off his food... 'Would you mind if I took it to him?' she requested persuasively. 'I need to talk to him about a few things, anyway,' she added lightly.

Mrs Graham gave a mischievous smile even as she nodded. 'He's less likely to shout at you,' she explained ruefully.

Skye picked up the tray. 'I wouldn't be too sure of that, if I were you!'

'Go on with you!' the housekeeper teased. 'You'll find him in his study,' she added helpfully.

Skye's own smile faded as soon as she had left the kitchen with the tray, her nervousness returning as she slowly made her way to Falkner's study.

What was she going to say to him? How could she even begin to broach the subject that was dearest to her heart? She certainly couldn't just blurt out that she had changed her mind about marrying him! That would be—

That was it! Falkner's marriage proposal! That was what had been niggling at the back of her mind these last few days!

Her strides towards Falkner's study were more purposeful now, Skye knowing exactly what her first question to Falkner was going to be!

The door to his study stood slightly ajar, giving Skye the opportunity to look at him for several seconds without his being aware of her presence.

His expression was bleak rather than grim as he stared out of the window beside his desk, his face pale with strain, the lines beside his eyes and mouth seeming to have deepened since he'd first burst back into her life over a week ago.

If she had been unhappy these last few days, then Falkner didn't look as if he had fared any better!

She took a deep breath, building up the nerve for this confrontation with Falkner. Because she had no doubt that was what this was going to be!

Unable to knock on the door to announce her entrance because both hands were occupied in carrying the tray, Skye nudged the door open with her foot before striding into the room. 'Mrs Graham thought you might like some soup,' she announced brightly, having the satisfaction of seeing the total shock flare in Falkner's briefly unguarded expression at her completely unexpected appearance in his study.

Brief, because Falkner quickly had his emotions under control, straightening slowly in his chair to look at her with narrowed eyes. 'What are you doing here?'

'I told you, delivering soup.' She put the tray down pointedly on his bare desktop. So much for his excuse of not being able to join his family for dinner because he had 'calls to make'!

His mouth twisted derisively. 'That isn't what I meant, and you know it.'

Skye shrugged. 'Nevertheless, I have brought you some soup. Mrs Graham tells me you've been off your food just recently,' she added lightly.

His expression tightened. 'Does she indeed?' he muttered disapprovingly.

'She does.' Skye nodded, outwardly appearing much more confident than she actually felt inside; her legs didn't feel too steady, and her palms were damp with nervousness! 'Would you mind if I sat down?' She arched auburn brows.

'Be my guest,' he invited dryly. 'You can eat the soup, if you would like it,' he added dismissively.

'No, thanks,' she refused, sinking gratefully into the chair opposite his desk. 'My appetite seems to have deserted me just recently, too,' she added ruefully.

Falkner continued to look at her with that narrowed gaze, but, from the scowl that deepened between his eyes, he didn't feel in the least reassured by what he saw in Skye's face.

'This is all very pleasant, Skye,' he bit out with obvious impatience. 'But shouldn't you be sitting down to dinner with Belinda and Charles?'

'Probably.' She nodded, wishing she could read more from his expression; just a glimmer of pleasure at her unexpected presence here would be enough to help her through this conversation! But she was out of luck: Falkner's expression completely—deliberately?—unreadable. 'But there was something I wanted to ask you,' she added determinedly.

'And it couldn't wait until tomorrow?' he taunted.

'No, it couldn't,' she snapped irritably, glaring across at him. He certainly wasn't making this easy for her!

'Well?' he prompted impatiently when she made no effort to continue.

Skye moistened dry lips, wondering, now that she was actually facing Falkner, if Belinda couldn't be wrong, if she weren't about to make a fool of herself, after all. But what did she really have to lose? Besides, there was still that nagging inconsistency concerning the timing of Falkner's marriage proposal...

She drew in a deep breath, forcing herself to meet the steadiness of his gaze; she didn't have anything to lose, but if she was right—if!—then she had everything to win. 'Falkner, why did you ask me to marry you?'

At that moment she was glad she had refused to drop her gaze from his, otherwise she might have missed that sudden blaze of emotion in his eyes, an emotion that was quickly masked but that she had seen anyway.

Her own eyes widened expectantly as she waited for his answer.

CHAPTER FOURTEEN

FALKNER stood up restlessly, wearing faded blue denims and a light blue shirt now in preference to the suit he had been wearing earlier, the slight awkwardness of his right leg emphasised this evening too, testament to his tiredness.

This evidence of his tiredness pulled at Skye's heart-strings, and it took every ounce of her will-power not to say something. That, and the fact that she knew she would only be inviting a cutting comment from Falkner if she so much as dared to mention his past injury.

'Well?' she finally prompted in much the same way he had seconds earlier.

His mouth tightened ominously. 'Surely it's obvious why,' he snapped dismissively. 'Besides, we've moved on from there—'

'I haven't,' Skye cut in quickly; he wasn't going to change the subject that easily! 'And it isn't obvious at all, Falkner,' she continued evenly. 'At least, not to me. At the time you asked me to marry you I believed it was out of pity for my suddenly fath—' She drew in a deeply con-trolling breath. 'For my fatherless, moneyless state—'

'And so it was,' Falkner confirmed impatiently.

'Rubbish!' she sharply repeated Belinda's rebuke of a short time ago. 'Okay, I accept that the first part of that statement may be true,' she murmured huskily. 'But the second part certainly wasn't,' she came back strongly. 'And, as one of my trustees, you knew that it wasn't,' she added pointedly.

That was the 'something' that had kept niggling at her subconscious, the 'something' that didn't quite add up, the 'something' she had been too upset to make sense of for four days, the 'something' she so desperately needed an answer to now. Because Falkner had known that in only seven months' time she would inherit the money from her trust fund, that she would then be a wealthy young lady, that she had no need of a protector, financial or otherwise...

Falkner frowned darkly. 'I—you—'

'Yes?' she prompted tensely, sitting forward on her seat as she looked up at him expectantly, reassured by this suddenly speechless Falkner.

His expression became derisive. 'Have you ever thought of becoming a lawyer, Skye? Because you certainly have the aggressive style of a prosecution lawyer!' he added mockingly.

He was trying to change the subject, and Skye refused to let him.

'No, I haven't,' she dismissed impatiently. 'Now would you please answer the question?'

He shook his head. 'I've forgotten what it was.'

Somehow, she didn't think so! 'Why did you ask me to marry you?' she repeated evenly.

He thrust his hands deep into the pockets of his denims, his shoulders hunched defensively. 'Why do you think I asked you?' he finally murmured slowly.

'If I knew that I wouldn't be here asking you!' she came back frustratedly.

He really didn't want to answer this question, did he? Could it possibly be for the reason she had thought—hoped? Skye was still too uncertain of the answer to dare to hope too deeply…!

He gave a deep sigh, shaking his head. 'Whether you want to believe it or not, I did feel sorry for you. Not only because of your father, but because of what I had just learnt about your uncle Seamus too. I wanted—' He broke off, breathing heavily. 'I just wanted to take care of you!' he finished frustratedly.

Skye frowned. 'Why?'

'Because you were alone. Because of my friendship for your father. Because—'

'Did you marry Selina for those reasons too?' Skye cut in determinedly, standing up too now to face him unflinchingly as he stood only feet away from her. 'Or did you marry her because she was like me?' she added huskily.

There, she had said it now, had said what Belinda had been implying earlier, and what Skye herself had concluded after looking at the photograph album. Heaven help her if they were both wrong!

Falkner's expression darkened, his eyes blazing silver in the paleness of his face. 'Selina was absolutely nothing like you!' he rasped coldly. 'Nothing!' he added forcefully.

Skye flinched at the vehemence in his tone. Did he mean that Selina was so much more than her, or did he mean the opposite? She simply didn't know!

That uncertainty kept her rooted to the spot as Falkner stepped forward to grasp her by the tops of her arms. 'Why are you asking me these things, Skye?' Falkner demanded bleakly, shaking her slightly.

'Don't you know?' she choked, her eyes bright with unshed tears. 'Don't you really know, Falkner?'

A nerve pulsed in his rigidly clenched jaw as he became suddenly still, his gaze searching now. 'Tell me,' he finally invited huskily.

She swallowed hard. 'I'm asking—I'm asking for the sake of a young almost-eighteen-year-old girl who fell in love with you six years ago!' she blurted out, beyond caution now, beyond anything but telling Falkner how she felt. And if he rejected her, if she was wrong and he didn't care for her after all, then she would have to live with that! 'I'm asking for the sake of the almost-twenty-five-year-old young woman who is still in love with you!' she added brokenly.

If he should turn her away now—if he should—

'Dear heaven!' Falkner groaned emotionally, staring down at her disbelievingly, his hands having tightened painfully on her arms. 'Skye...?'

'Falkner...!' she came back achingly, the tears spilling hotly over her lashes now to fall unheeded down her cheeks.

Please, she pleaded inwardly as he continued to stare at her incredulously. Oh, please...!

'You love me?' he repeated huskily.

She nodded. 'I always have. I always will,' she added with a certainty that allowed no quarter.

'Dear heaven...!' he repeated achingly before gathering her up in his arms and crushing her to his chest. 'Skye!' he groaned emotionally, his face buried in her hair.

She wasn't wrong. She couldn't be wrong!

Her own arms moved up about his waist as she pressed even closer against him. How she loved this man!

Falkner moved back slightly, his hands moving up to

cradle either side of her face as he looked down at her. 'You have the courage of a lioness,' he murmured admiringly. 'I'm not sure I could have done what you just did,' he explained huskily at her questioning look. 'But I'm very glad that you did!' he added fervently, bending his head to kiss her lingeringly on the lips. 'I love you, Skye O'Hara,' he told her forcefully. 'I always have. I always will,' he echoed her own vow of seconds ago.

'Oh, Falkner!' she groaned brokenly. 'How much time we've wasted!'

'But no more,' he declared firmly. 'Marry me, Skye. Marry me, and make my life complete!'

'Gladly!' she assured him emotionally, her own lips parting now as Falkner began to kiss her.

She had come home. Neither Ireland nor England was where she belonged; wherever this man was, whatever he was, whatever he became, that was where she wanted to be!

She melted against him, their two bodies melding into one, the two halves of a perfect whole.

'You've let your soup get cold,' Skye murmured a long time later, sitting on Falkner's knee as the two of them now occupied the chair behind his desk. 'Mrs Graham isn't going to be pleased,' she added teasingly.

Falkner smiled down at her, one of his hands playing with the silky fire of her hair. 'Mrs Graham will forgive me once she knows you're going to be my wife.' His smile faded, his arms tightening about her. 'I'll never let you go now, Skye, you do realize that?'

She looked up at him with sleepy satiation. 'From now on, Falkner, you'll have trouble going anywhere without me. "Wither thou goest", and all that,' she added self-consciously, still shaken as to how much she had realized she needed him. After years of believing Falkner would never be hers, the thought now of ever being away from him filled her with desolation.

'And all that,' Falkner echoed firmly. 'I only feel completely alive when I'm with you, Skye, feel as if I've merely existed for the last six and a half years.'

Skye turned to him frowningly. 'The last six and a half years…? But, Falkner—'

'I fell in love with you the first time I met you,' he admitted shakily. 'Of course, I tried to deny it, even to myself; after all, you weren't quite eighteen, and I was a worldly-wise thirty-two-year-old,' he acknowledged grimly. 'The whole idea was ridiculous, was what I told myself. Or else it was premature senility setting in,' he added self-derisively. 'I couldn't possibly have fallen in love with someone I had just met, let alone a baby like you!'

Skye reached up to caress the smoothness of his cheek, revelling in the freedom to be allowed such intimacies. 'But you had,' she prompted softly.

'Oh, yes.' He nodded grimly. 'After weeks of hell, when I tried to deny the truth even to myself—when I lost three straight competitions in a row, I'll have you know!— I knew I was just wasting my time trying to do any such thing. Why do you think I sent Storm to you, after all, if it wasn't in the hope that I might hear from you again— if only to ask me why I had changed my mind?'

'I had no idea!' Her eyes widened incredulously. 'And I was so stunned by his arrival, so tied up in knots at the fact that I had fallen in love with you, that I didn't even write you a thank-you letter!'

'No.' He grimaced at the memory. 'But I was glad

you had Storm anyway, hoped that you might occasionally think of me—and think of me kindly,' he added
self-derisively.

'I've thought of nothing else but you for six years!'
she told him forcefully. 'When I saw your engagement,
and then wedding, in the newspapers, I thought I was
going to die!' Her eyes became haunted by the memory
of her complete desolation five years ago.

'Oh, Skye!' He buried his face in her throat, breathing in her perfume, the warmth that was her, like a dying
man gasping for air. 'Marrying Selina was the biggest—
and most selfish!—mistake of my life.' He straightened,
shaking his head. 'I met her at some party or other of
Belinda's.' His eyes were bleak as he looked into the
past. 'The only thing about her that I really saw was her
resemblance to you. The only thing I wanted to see, I
think,' he added heavily. 'We were actually in church,
signing the register, when I finally realized exactly what
I was doing, that the woman standing beside me was a
stranger. By which time, it was too late,' he concluded
self-disgustedly.

Skye felt a shiver down her spine at the finality of
those words, the fact that both she and Belinda had been
right in their surmise doing nothing to alleviate the
sadness that she felt for Selina and Falkner; in the circumstances Falkner was describing, their marriage had
never stood a chance of succeeding.

'I was completely unfair to Selina,' Falkner continued determinedly. 'Is it any wonder, under the circumstances I've described, that she looked to other men to
give her the love and attention I was incapable of giving
her? I did try, Skye, I really did, knew that I owed it to
Selina to try and make it work. But it was no good; we

were more or less separated anyway, by the time I had the accident, and in the circumstances I thought it best to let her divorce me. She's happily remarried now with a baby son,' he added thankfully.

Skye moistened her lips. 'There were rumours—it was said—'

'That there was another woman?' Falkner finished wryly. 'That was you, Skye. I told you, it's always been you.' His eyes glowed with that love as he looked at her.

Her eyes widened. 'You told Selina about me?' He had told his wife, when Skye herself hadn't even known how he felt about her…?

He shook his head. 'I didn't have to. Skye, between a husband and wife—there can't be those sort of secrets.' He sighed heavily. 'I didn't want her, Skye,' he explained gruffly. 'I couldn't—I didn't feel that way about her—our marriage was a sham almost from start to finish!'

Skye could only stare at him as the full import of his words became clear to her.

'I may be many things, Skye, and my behaviour towards Selina was despicable, but after the first few months I knew I couldn't continue to live a lie,' he added heavily.

It seemed incredible to Skye that the marriage had lasted as long as it had. But she knew exactly what Falkner meant about it being a lie to pretend to care for someone else. It was because she felt that way herself that she had made the claim that she would never marry; if she couldn't be with Falkner, then she didn't want to be with anyone…

'It was a living hell, Skye,' Falkner continued at her silence. 'I was living with one woman, while in love with another one. It was a relief to us both, I think, when it finally broke down altogether. If it hadn't been for Connor—'

'My father knew about all this?' Skye gasped.

Falkner grimaced. 'Not that I was in love with you, no. But he was very supportive during that disruptive time of my life, and as a consequence the two of us became good friends.' He shrugged. 'But can you imagine your father's horror if I had ever admitted to him it was his cherished only daughter I was in love with?'

Skye wasn't so sure her father would have been horrified... After all, he had chosen Falkner, of all people, to be one of her trustees. Perhaps if there had been more time, if her father hadn't died, he might even have tried, in his own inimitable style, to get the two of them together. Skye liked to think so.

Falkner sighed. 'Of course, I wished things had been different, but after the accident, my long convalescence, and subsequent divorce, it had become an impossible situation. Your father apart, there was no way I could ever even consider asking you to marry me, a man so much older than you, who was crippled and divorced into the bargain!' Falkner murmured huskily.

'It wouldn't have mattered to me,' she told him intensely.

He gave a self-derisive grimace. 'But I didn't know that! Skye, the last three years have been absolute hell, believing, after the mess I had made of my life, that I stood absolutely no chance with you. You asked me once why, if I was such a good friend of your father's, you hadn't seen me during the last six months?' He sighed as she nodded slowly. 'If you remember, I told you you were mistaken, that I had seen him, that I had seen you too?'

She swallowed hard, clearly remembering that conversation. 'Yes.'

He nodded. 'You were in London with Connor three months ago, and you came to meet your father after a business meeting at a hotel there. Skye, I was the person Connor was meeting that day, and I watched from a hotel window as the two of you met outside in the street.'

Which was why he had shown no surprise by her changed appearance when he'd come to the hospital last week—her extra slenderness and short hair; he had already known of those changes because he had seen her!

'Over the last three years I've seen you five times under similar circumstances,' he added huskily.

'Falkner, I think you're wrong about my father not knowing how you felt about me,' she insisted slowly. 'He had no idea how I felt about you, certainly, because I had done such a good job over the years of hiding it from him,' she admitted self-derisively. 'But I don't believe for a moment that he didn't realize exactly who it was you were in love with. He talked about you to me several times,' she admitted ruefully. 'And on each of those occasions I was the one to change the subject, giving the deliberate impression that I wasn't in the least interested in anything to do with you.'

She really did believe that her father wholeheartedly approved of Falkner as a husband for her, felt more positive than ever, after listening to what Falkner had just said, that her father would never have entrusted her future to a man he didn't have complete trust in himself. In every way.

'He's probably out there somewhere right now smiling at the rightness of all this,' she continued huskily. 'So I'll ask you again, Falkner.' She straightened, looking at him intently. 'Why did you ask me to marry you on Friday?'

His expression softened, his eyes glittering emotionally. 'Because I love you more than life itself. Because I thought I might be able to persuade you into marriage in a weak moment. Because I hoped that once we were married I might one day be able to persuade you into loving me. Because the thought of you going out of my life a second time is more than I can bear. Because—'

'Enough.' She placed gentle fingertips over his lips. 'I'll marry you, Falkner, but only because all the things you've just said about me could as easily be said of me concerning you! You'll never know how tempted I was to accept your proposal in the hope that one day you might learn to love me! Isn't it wonderful that we already love each other?' Her eyes misted with tears of happiness.

'Wonderful!' Falkner echoed emotionally.

Thank you, Da, Skye offered up a silent prayer even as she and Falkner kissed each other as if they never wanted to stop. Thank you. Thank you!

EPILOGUE

'WHAT are you doing?'

Skye turned to smile at Falkner as he stood in the stable doorway, her love for him glowing in her eyes.

The last year of being married to Falkner had been the happiest of her life, the two of them rarely apart, enjoying their silences together as much as they did their chats, the teasing repartee that had become such a part of their relationship. As for their lovemaking… Falkner had been perfectly correct in his claim that the damage to his right leg wasn't noticeable when he was 'lying horizontal'!

Skye put her arms about his waist to hug him tight as he joined her in Storm's stall. 'I was just explaining to Storm that he'll have to be put out to pasture for a while,' she murmured softly.

'He will?' Falkner looked surprised, knowing how much she enjoyed those daily rides out on Storm, often joining her on his own mare, the stallion seeming to have accepted that this man was now a permanent fixture in his mistress's life. At least, he no longer tried to bite Falkner!

'Yes.' Skye smiled shyly up at her husband. 'Of course I've explained to him that it's only until after the baby is born.' She held her breath as she looked up to gauge Falkner's reaction to her news.

The two of them were so happy together, enjoyed being together so much, that the subject of children had just never arisen. But she had had her suspicions for the last couple of weeks, and a visit to the doctor that morning had confirmed those suspicions: she and Falkner were to have a baby in the spring.

A little boy, she had wondered dreamily on her drive back from the doctor, with Falkner's blond hair and aristocratic features. Or maybe a little girl, with Skye's own red flaming hair.

'Skye!' Falkner cried ecstatically as he gathered her fiercely into his arms, instantly slackening his hold as he realized he was crushing her. 'Is it true?' His eyes glowed with pleasure. 'Are you sure?'

'The doctor is—which is more important.' She relaxed into his arms, having no doubts now that his reaction to her news was definitely positive.

'I never thought—I can hardly believe—' He shook his head. 'Skye, I didn't believe I could possibly be any happier than I am already, but this! Are you pleased?' He looked down at her concernedly.

'Ecstatic,' she assured him unhesitantly. 'I can imagine nothing more wonderful than having our child,' she added emotionally.

'Neither can I.' Falkner gathered her into his arms once more. 'If it's a boy we'll call him Connor, after your father.'

Skye felt that familiar emotional lump in her throat as she thought of her beloved da.

Thank you, Da; she again offered up a silent prayer. Thank you for giving me Falkner. And thank you for giving me to Falkner.

EXTRA

FORCED TO MARRY

Wives for the taking!

Once these men put a diamond ring on their bride's
finger, there's no going back....

Wedlocked and willful, these wives will get a
wedding night they'll never forget!

**Read all the fantastic stories, out this month
in Harlequin Presents EXTRA:**

The Santangeli Marriage #61
by SARA CRAVEN

Salzano's Captive Bride #62
by DAPHNE CLAIR

**The Ruthless Italian's
Inexperienced Wife** #63
by CHRISTINA HOLLIS

Bought for Marriage #64
by MARGARET MAYO

HPE0709

HARLEQUIN *Presents*

International Billionaires

Life is a game of power and pleasure.
And these men play to win!

THE SHEIKH'S LOVE-CHILD
by *Kate Hewitt*

When Lucy arrives in the desert kingdom of Biryal,
Sheikh Khaled's eyes are blacker and harder than
before. But Lucy and the sheikh are inextricably
bound forever—for he is the father of her son....

Book #2838

Available July 2009

Two more titles to collect in this exciting miniseries:
BLACKMAILED INTO THE GREEK
TYCOON'S BED by *Carol Marinelli*
August

THE VIRGIN SECRETARY'S
IMPOSSIBLE BOSS by *Carole Mortimer*
September

www.eHarlequin.com HP12838

HARLEQUIN *Presents*

TWO CROWNS, TWO ISLANDS, ONE LEGACY

A royal family, torn apart by pride and its lust for power, reunited by purity and passion

THE ROYAL HOUSE *of* KAREDES

coming in 2009

BILLIONAIRE PRINCE, PREGNANT MISTRESS
by Sandra Marton, July

THE PLAYBOY SHEIKH'S VIRGIN STABLE-GIRL
by Sharon Kendrick, August

THE PRINCE'S CAPTIVE WIFE
by Marion Lennox, September

THE SHEIKH'S FORBIDDEN VIRGIN
by Kate Hewitt, October

THE GREEK BILLIONAIRE'S
INNOCENT PRINCESS
by Chantelle Shaw, November

THE FUTURE KING'S LOVE-CHILD
by Melanie Milburne, December

RUTHLESS BOSS, ROYAL MISTRESS
by Natalie Anderson, January

THE DESERT KING'S HOUSEKEEPER BRIDE
by Carol Marinelli, February

8 volumes to collect and treasure!

www.eHarlequin.com

HP12835

I ♥ HARLEQUIN® *Presents*

BROUGHT TO YOU BY FANS OF
HARLEQUIN PRESENTS.

We are its editors and authors
and biggest fans—and we'd
love to hear from YOU!

Subscribe today to our online blog at
www.iheartpresents.com

REQUEST YOUR FREE BOOKS!

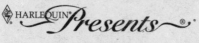 HARLEQUIN *Presents*

PASSION GUARANTEED SEDUCTION

2 FREE NOVELS PLUS 2 FREE GIFTS!

YES! Please send me 2 FREE Harlequin Presents® novels and my 2 FREE gifts (gifts are worth about $10). After receiving them, if I don't wish to receive any more books, I can return the shipping statement marked "cancel". If I don't cancel, I will receive 6 brand-new novels every month and be billed just $4.05 per book in the U.S. or $4.74 per book in Canada. That's a savings of close to 15% off the cover price! It's quite a bargain! Shipping and handling is just 50¢ per book*. I understand that accepting the 2 free books and gifts places me under no obligation to buy anything. I can always return a shipment and cancel at any time. Even if I never buy another book, the two free books and gifts are mine to keep forever.

106 HDN EYRQ   306 HDN EYR2

Name	(PLEASE PRINT)
Address	Apt. #
City	State/Prov.	Zip/Postal Code

Signature (if under 18, a parent or guardian must sign)

Mail to the **Harlequin Reader Service:**
IN U.S.A.: P.O. Box 1867, Buffalo, NY 14240-1867
IN CANADA: P.O. Box 609, Fort Erie, Ontario L2A 5X3

Not valid to current subscribers of Harlequin Presents books.

Are you a current subscriber of Harlequin Presents books and want to receive the larger-print edition? Call 1-800-873-8635 today!

* Terms and prices subject to change without notice. Prices do not include applicable taxes. Sales tax applicable in N.Y. Canadian residents will be charged applicable provincial taxes and GST. Offer not valid in Quebec. This offer is limited to one order per household. All orders subject to approval. Credit or debit balances in a customer's account(s) may be offset by any other outstanding balance owed by or to the customer. Please allow 4 to 6 weeks for delivery. Offer available while quantities last.

Your Privacy: Harlequin Books is committed to protecting your privacy. Our Privacy Policy is available online at www.eHarlequin.com or upon request from the Reader Service. From time to time we make our lists of customers available to reputable third parties who may have a product or service of interest to you. If you would prefer we not share your name and address, please check here. ☐

HP09R

You're invited to join our Tell Harlequin Reader Panel!

By joining our new reader panel you will:

- Receive Harlequin® books—they are FREE and yours to keep with no obligation to purchase anything!
- Participate in fun online surveys
- Exchange opinions and ideas with women just like you
- Have a say in our new book ideas and help us publish the best in women's fiction

In addition, you will have a chance to win great prizes and receive special gifts!
See Web site for details. Some conditions apply.
Space is limited.

To join, visit us at
www.TellHarlequin.com.